FATE'S CRUEL CRY

BRIAN DE LA COUR

Copyright © 2019 by Brian De La Cour

All rights reserved.

No part of this book may be reproduced in any form or by any electronic or mechanical means, including information storage and retrieval systems, without written permission from the author, except for the use of brief quotations in a book review.

This book is a work of fiction. Names, characters, businesses, organisations, places, events and incidents either are the product of the author's imagination or are used fictitiously. Any resemblance to actual persons, living or dead, events or locales is entirely coincidental.

Book and cover design by Sharn Hutton.

First edition September 2019.

10 9 8 7 6 5 4 3 2

For my wife Dora, who never stopped believing.

1

Life is likened to a path which narrows and widens through pain or euphoria. The path may be long or the path may be short as defined by destiny. Its course cannot be altered and its end may be distant or near.

– Thoughts of a holy man.

Isaiah Stiener was born in Charleston, West Virginia, on the sixth of June at six a.m. in the year 1810.

Ernestine Stiener was built for child bearing being short, stocky and broad of rump and hip. All her pregnancies had been easy and Isaiah's was no exception.

Giving birth in the squatting position, much to the local midwife's disapproval, he slid from her womb and the tract of birth with ease.

After mopping perspiration from her flushed cheeks Ernestine cradled her new born; a boy, after a succession of five daughters, all of whom jostled round their mother's bed eager to take their first glimpse of their baby brother. They giggled and squealed at his swarthy little body; his surprising shock of fair hair, and his tiny wrinkled face. They gasped at the unusual volume of his cry, the power of his lungs, and the intensity of his wide blue eyes.

Ernestine's husband, Peter Stiener, was the son of an Austrian immigrant; a graduate of theology, who eventually became ordained within the Methodist ministry.

Ernestine had married him mainly for reasons of financial security. Her upbringing had been middle class, however her father had faced ruin due to heavy gambling debts and had taken his whole family down with him. He was discovered with the barrel of a flintlock pistol fused to the roof of his mouth in a blood-splattered study, the back of his head blown to fragments.

Peter Stiener was a relatively wealthy man, having inherited his father's shares in the local salt mining industry; and with the aid of some of that wealth he became one of the founding fathers of the new Methodist chapel in Charleston and eventually became its pastor.

His views had their roots in old-style Puritanism and his weekly sermons invariably focused on God's judgement. He was a powerful and magnetic orator and preached without notes to full congregations every Sunday; and women had been known to scream and faint at the fervour of his delivery; and it was rumoured that there were times when mesmerised parishioners confessed to sensing the sulphur of Hell. Driven by fanaticism he was addicted to the adrenalin of whipping up the emotions of his congregation and using the threat of God's judgement to engender fear and thereby enhance his own kudos.

He believed implicitly in the force of evil and performed numerous exorcisms and the casting out of demons. One such exorcism resulted in the death of a young girl from a violent seizure; however, such was Peter Stiener's influence and standing in the local community that the coroner ruled that no inquiry was necessary, and that the child had died from natural causes.

Many would have called Peter Stiener handsome. His yellow hair was wiry and close-cropped; his complexion fair and freckled. He was powerfully built with a bull neck and his gaze was penetrating.

There was, however, a dark side to his psyche. He

was prone to violent rages and his conviction was that his every thought and deed was a manifestation of the power of the divine.

This delusional state of mind had resulted in a void of conscience. He led a virtual double life in which he would indulge with impunity in acts of debauchery.

There were times when he would leave Ernestine and his daughters and be gone for days. He would frequent brothels, taverns and roadhouses, riding for miles across country. He would return dishevelled, wild-eyed and tormented by inner voices, and lock himself in his study.

Then after a while could be heard the sufferance of his penance; first a rant, begging forgiveness, then the panting masturbatory groan of self-flagellation.

Ernestine knew better than to inquire as to his whereabouts for days on end; she suffered him with stoical patience.

Ernestine brought up her daughters, cooked, cleaned and organised her household with the help of Clara Meek, an orphaned girl whom the Stieners had taken in as a housekeeper not long after they were married. Ernestine adored Clara, indeed they were close, almost sisterly and to contemplate life without Clara was unthinkable; she brightened Ernestine's days, and her companionship gave Ernestine the strength of purpose to endure the egomania of her husband. Her five daughters also regarded Clara with deep affection.

For all his faults Peter Stiener provided well for his family. His daughters were well-fed, well-dressed and well-mannered. After five daughters, Peter Stiener had despaired of ever being blessed with a son. He longed for a son; a son to continue the Stiener name and also a son who in Peter's mind would without question follow him in his ministry. So when the news of Isaiah's birth reached him he basked in a glow of satisfaction and made plans immediately for his son's future.

Being the only boy, Isaiah was cosseted and adored by his mother and all his sisters. However, by contrast, his later childhood years were blighted by regular theological discourses and Bible readings with his father behind a locked study door, during which Peter Stiener conducted coercive grooming sessions with his son in order to establish a mind-set that replicated his own.

Peter Stiener's bellowing voice could often be heard from within his study whenever Isaiah attempted to interject with the slightest contrary statement or question.

Peter Stiener's regard for his son became that of a commodity that would safeguard the perpetuation of his ministry, and the notion of treating Isaiah with any form of love or affection did not figure in his psyche.

However, even at such a young age, Isaiah did possess strength of character and of mind, and by dint of its process, his father's attempts at indoctrination did eventually create in him a reverse attitude of latent rebellion.

In the year 1827, at the age of seventeen, and without any discussion or consultation, Peter Stiener enrolled his son at the Academy of St John the Devine. Isaiah had absolutely no say in the matter, he would attend or incur his father's extreme displeasure.

It was a fee-paying institution run by middle-aged biblical scholars, and it was intended as a place of preliminary learning for young males with ambitions of becoming theologians or entering the priesthood. It offered a curriculum of both theological and academic studies. The students at the college consisted of a mixture of borders and day attenders of which Isaiah was one. Clara drove Isaiah the nine miles each morning to the academy in the family buggy and also collected him each evening at the end of lectures.

By this time all of Isaiah's sisters had made their own way in the world. All were attractive young women and it could be said that three of them were undoubtedly beautiful.

Adina, the eldest, had moved to New York and entered the teaching profession. She remained a spinster.

Bethel had joined a local law firm as an accounting clerk, had fallen in love with one of the partners, and they had married.

Tirzah and Zemina had married twin brothers, heirs to a large coffee importing company, and had settled in San Francisco.

Bethany had married the local gunsmith.

Of all his sisters, Bethany was undoubtedly Isaiah's favourite.

A strapping girl of almost six feet, she was the most physical of all the girls, preferring outdoor activities like riding, log-splitting, and shooting game, to the more traditional middle class female pursuits of embroidery, music, drawing and book collecting. She and Isaiah were both natural makers and they would often be found together in the rear outhouse and wood store fashioning artefacts from wood.

Bethany was a vivacious, contented girl with a near perpetual smile and a raucous infectious laugh.

Her fascination with the craft of the gunsmith led her to form a relationship with the local gunmaker, with whom she ultimately fell in love. Bethany's husband Caitlin was the son of an Irish immigrant and gunsmith who had died unexpectedly some years earlier. The business then passed to Caitlin whom for years had been apprentice to the trade.

Caitlin was a quiet, wiry, slim man, slightly shorter than Bethany and a year older.

Many had commented that he and Bethany were an unlikely match, however their marriage remained strong.

Isaiah's sisters had married well and it could be said, were financially secure. However, the good men they had married were blissfully unaware of the tawdry hypocritical double life that their father-in-law was leading, and eventually Peter Stiener reaped what he had sewn, and the price he paid for his excessive debauchery was high.

A short while after an encounter with a seasoned middle-aged prostitute he became aware of a lesion at the base of his penis.

Over a period of weeks the lesion increased in size, began to weep and became chronic.

For a man of Peter Stiener's learning he possessed surprising ignorance of the venereal repercussions of promiscuity and he thought nothing more of it, when eventually the lesion healed and disappeared; Syphilis, however, had left its calling card.

Ernestine was in no danger of being infected; she no longer slept with her husband. Indeed, relations had grown so cold between them, they barely exchanged words, and virtually led separate lives.

They were seen together only when Peter delivered his Sunday sermons.

Peter Stiener took it for granted that Isaiah would excel at theological academy and thoroughly enjoy his time there. He was never more wrong.

During his time at the academy a rift would fester between father and son; a rift that eventually would become a chasm of hatred and animosity that would shape their future for years to come.

After one month Isaiah showed little sign of settling in. He detested the gloomy, grey aspect of the building and the musty chalk and boiled greens odour of the corridors, and was at constant loggerheads with a number of the college tutors.

He displayed ability, in English and drawing, was a fine sportsman, struggled with all other academic subjects, and disagreed profoundly with religious instruction and the views and opinions propounded by the ancient, out of touch theologians who taught it. The more intimidating dictatorial dogma was served up each week, the more Isaiah spoke out against it, and the more he considered it an infringement of freedom of thought and an individual's right to choose. Such was the extent of his rebellious attitude that letters were written to his father with concerns over his lack of reverence, resulting in the occasional violent altercation.

Isaiah was an introvert who shied away from social gatherings, always preferring his own company. He was a deep thinker, and by choice an isolated individual who was the antithesis of gregariousness. He did not form relationships, not because he found it difficult, but because he did not want to.

Consequently, his isolationism caused some consternation amongst other members of his group at the academy.

Two boys in particular, one called Armitage and the other Bowman, found Isaiah's desire to keep himself to himself particularly irksome.

"Hey Stiener," said Bowman one morning. "What goes through that mind of yours?"

"My thoughts should be of no concern of yours," replied Isaiah in a low voice.

Irritated by the rebuff, Bowman continued.

"We are all training here to be future men of God; good fellowship and communication must be part of our calling, two things that you seem to ignore."

"I am not here out of choice, I attend this academy under duress; I do not believe any form of

God exists, and I will never be a man of God, as you call it."

Then eavesdropping, Armitage interjected: "Who do you think you are, Stiener? I don't like your arrogance. You clearly think that you're something special with your heretic and rebellious notions."

"Like I said, my ideas and attitudes are of no concern of yours or Bowman's," Isaiah countered, again in a low voice.

As the days went by, Armitage and Bowman's tirade toward Isaiah continued until Armitage's verbal bullying became physical, shoving Isaiah backwards as he berated him. This ultimately became too much for Isaiah and his patience finally snapped, and Armitage received a hairline fracture to his cheekbone for his troubles.

After this, realising that Isaiah meant business, the two eventually backed off and the three made an attempt at a silent but uncomfortable co-existence, and any enquiries by academy staff as to the reason for Armitage's facial bruising were honourably lied about in accordance with an unwritten code.

Sometime later Isaiah's generally miserable existence was exacerbated even further by a disturbing occurrence involving English master Felix Myers.

A list of names was attached to the classroom wall requesting that the boys on the list, of which Isaiah was one, attend revision tutorials once a week, after hours, with Felix Myers in his study. Isaiah was puzzled. He was a high achiever in English and considered that he was in no need of additional tuition. He could identify other members of his class who were less advanced than he and were in need of revision. He studied the list further and came to the conclusion that the list had not been compiled in response to a student's lack of literary ability. Curious, this continued to dog his thoughts for some time.

Isaiah attended the first hour long tutorial in which Myers proceeded to discuss with great alacrity various grammatical aspects of selected passages of Williams Hill Brown's novel, *The Power of Sympathy*.

After the hour Myers complimented Isaiah on his efforts and then informed him that the tutorial had ended and that he could go.

Myers was a man in his mid-fifties, balding and overweight. His complexion was florid due to large patches of broken veins on his cheeks and nose. He was not without charm; his voice was deep and smooth, and he possessed powers of persuasion that he used to his advantage to achieve his own selfish ends.

Myers had also arranged for his tutorials to take place at the end of the boys' weekly cross-country run in anticipation that his study might become charged with the odour of male sweat and the testosterone of exertion.

After the first forty five minutes of the second

tutorial, and after locking his study door, Myers' advance was inappropriate and furtive. Isaiah recoiled at the closeness of his leer, his rank breath and clumsy groping with quivering fat fingers.

Myers wheezed and stammered with pursed lips.

"C-calm boy, calm boy!" as he edged closer, breathless and shuddering.

Isaiah froze, rendered temporarily immobile by shock and the mildly hypnotic effect of Myers' stare.

Then pulling back, he mumbled, "Good, good, tutorial over, remember same time next week, now get you gone."

Then, in a state of total disbelief at what had just occurred, Isaiah grabbed his bag and made for the door.

But before unlocking it Myers said, "Remember, boy, all will remain in these walls, otherwise there will be consequences, severe consequences for you, remember that, boy."

Isaiah then left Myers' study and made his way to the academy gates where, as always, Clara was waiting for him in the buggy. He disclosed nothing of the incident to Clara or anyone else.

He was disturbed by what had occurred for days after and the following week he arrived for the third tutorial feeling anxious and apprehensive.

He did consider disobeying Myers and not attending further tutorials, but then thought better of it, fearing that reports of his disobedience might reach his father.

Once again Myers locked his study door after Isaiah was seated, and once again they spent the first forty five minutes in text analysis.

Myers then began to fumble with himself under his gown, and again began to edge closer, his eyes wide, his expression fixed in a desire-induced leer; and once again the fat fingers began to grope.

"I could make things happen for you, boy, if perhaps we could come to future arrangements."

Then seized by sheer revulsion Isaiah took hold of Myers' groping wrist and forced it back; and with his other hand went for Myers' throat and squeezed.

Myers began to groan, saliva oozing from his lips.

"If and when your God judges you, Doctor Myers, how will you deal with your shame?"

Isaiah's voice was cold, low and faltering with rage.

"Swear to me that these filthy advances will stop. Swear!" he barked, tightening his grip on Myers' throat.

A shocked and choking Myers, so used to coaxing boys into submission, now began to tremble and with a faint trickle from his bladder, bulging eyes, face aflame, and his temples pulsating, he nodded meekly and mumbled, "I, I swear!"

And with that Isaiah released his grip with a thrust, jerking Myers' head back in the process. He then gathered his books, unlocked the study door and left a humiliated Myers sitting in his urine-soaked chair.

No repercussions occurred as a result and the following week Isaiah learned that all future revision tutorials had been cancelled.

After the incident Myers endeavoured to avoid Isaiah at every opportunity, and when they passed in the academy cloisters, Myers would look away, stony-faced, and briskly walk on.

Gifted with a fine voice, as a boy Isaiah had sung at his father's Sunday services, and later when his voice had broken he continued to sing as a powerful tenor.

His music tutor at the academy was an ex-parish priest and retired operatic tenor called Drummond.

A jovial, light-hearted and inspirational Irishman, Drummond was well-liked and for Isaiah his teaching was the single, most enjoyable and fulfilling activity in the dreary, oppressive academy.

Isaiah's voice blossomed under Drummond's instruction and in addition to practising the curriculum-specified statutory hymns, Drummond passed on the Gaelic folk songs and laments that he had learned as a youth in Ireland that were in his blood.

And accompanied by Drummond on the piano, Isaiah would occasionally sing the hymns at academy assemblies, and also, at the request of the

Dean, he would sing at special occasions in the academy great hall. And there were times when his singing was so inspired, and his tenor voice so sweet that, when he had sung there was rapturous applause, with hats tossed in the air and great cheers.

2

After eighteen months, aside from his fine and developing physical attributes, Isaiah's general mental malaise at the academy had worsened. His lack of reverence and opposition to the ethos of religious instruction had prompted the college governors to conclude that theology could never be his calling or vocation, and as a result letters were written to Peter Stiener urging him to remove Isaiah from their academy and transfer him to a totally secular institution.

As Isaiah matured he began to formulate a personal philosophy that was exclusively derived from pragmatic thought and proven theory, and as a result challenged concepts of spirituality and all forms of organised religion.

He constantly questioned the notion of God, the existence of whom he concluded could not be proven by any tangible evidence. He also questioned the notion of divine judgement that admitted the souls of the righteous to paradise and the souls of the sinful, and even the pure non-believer to eternal suffering.

To Isaiah, a process of rational deduction seemed to suggest that before the dawn of science the creation of the concept of God gave reason and explanation to the wonders of the Cosmos and that through history the fulcrums of power devised the reward of paradise and the tyranny of eternal damnation in an attempt to manipulate and instil social order. Surely God must only exist in the minds of men, he finally concluded.

He had been threatened with damnation many times whenever he dared incur his father's wrath and the more he rationalised his ideas and opinions, the more preposterous the concept of an afterlife became in relation to the logic of his thinking. Moreover, he wanted no truck with any religious order that produced odious predators like Myers and dictatorial fanatics like his father.

After Peter Stiener had received the governor's letter he demanded that Isaiah see him in his study. Isaiah was expecting a demented rant about dark forces being at work, followed up by a beating.

However, surprisingly, that was not Peter Stiener's reaction.

Instead he pulled Isaiah close to him by the collar and then eyeball to eyeball he calmly growled the following:

"You will continue your studies for which I have paid considerable fees and you will dispel all of your subversive and rebellious notions; and take on a more responsible and respectful attitude to the college and to me.

"I intend to write to the governors and inform them that your conduct is nothing more than irresponsible, ill-judged, youthful arrogance, and give them my word that you will become a dedicated, responsible scholar from this day forth, and finish your course of study, and make an attempt at some kind of union with God. Is that understood?"

Isaiah knew that to oppose his father in this mood would be futile, and so consequently he nodded, under a kind of duress, and left the study, his tail between his legs in a resultant state of depression.

In the ensuing months the relationship between Isaiah and Peter Stiener worsened, with increasing heated exchanges between the two often resulting in blows.

Ernestine could do nothing but be a helpless

onlooker. She believed Isaiah should be given freedom to form his own opinions and beliefs and her husband's violent, dictatorial rants only served to increase her contempt for him.

Misery, frustration and restlessness all combined to fuel Isaiah's desire to be free of his father's tyranny.

Disturbed sleep patterns became more frequent; a dream of running through a maze of dark, looming, saturated passages in a frantic search for an unknown entity or perhaps an unreachable truth would recur in different forms, and there were times when he would wake suddenly in a state of quasi consciousness and lay pulse pounding until gradually normal consciousness was regained.

In the morning he would strive to recall his night terror. Sometimes they were vivid and clear, and at other times they would fade quickly from his memory; and in an attempt to decipher and search for meaning he would struggle to interpret his dream sequences through drawn diagrams.

April marked the end of the second semester at the Academy of St John and Isaiah was driven home as usual by Clara in the buggy.

With each passing day Isaiah's increasing detestation of the place only served to make worse his generally depressed state of mind.

For some reason that evening Peter Stiener's mood was tetchy to say the least, and dinner was accompanied by a thundering lecture directed at Isaiah before Peter finally retired to his study.

After dinner Isaiah settled down in front of a crackling fire with his mother and Clara. He sported a bruised cheek from a previous altercation with his father, and staring at the glowing logs he became close to tears.

Ernestine threw her arms round him in an effort to comfort her son, and as they both gazed into the flames, the realisation and conclusion in both their minds was the inevitable; that Isaiah had no choice but to make a break from the impasse that had arisen between his father and himself.

The loss of her son would fill Ernestine with a lingering desolation, however she considered that her resultant sadness would be a small price to pay in order to prevent Isaiah's mental state from deteriorating even further, so consequently with Ernestine's blessing, it was decided that Isaiah should leave at the earliest opportunity.

He would time his leaving to coincide with one of his father's occasional excursions.

Conflict with his father apart, he felt a yearning for solitude, a nagging wanderlust, a desire for unrestricted freedom; a desire to be rid of the trappings of polite society, and God obsessed men going about their daily business.

He had read of the exploits of Lewis and Clark and the great frontier they had mapped; and also of accounts of the booming fur trade and of the trappers who forged a wild existence in the mountains and in Indian lands of the upper Missouri. All captured his imagination, and with each violent altercation with his father, his wanderlust had clawed deeper.

Isaiah informed Ernestine and Clara that he intended to head west.

Ernestine knew that she could never dampen the force of Isaiah's wanderlust, and she also feared an ultimate confrontation, the outcome of which could prove unthinkable should he continue to live under the same roof as his father and continue at the academy.

She would write to her elder brother Ernest, who ran a mercantile store in St Louis, and request that Isaiah might stay with him, and she would add that he would be willing to work in order to earn his keep.

Some weeks later a letter from St Louis arrived addressed to Ernestine. She recognised immediately the rough scrawled hand and the slightly soiled wax sealed parchment. It was a reply from Ernest and in it he stated that he would be only too pleased to have his nephew stay with him and what's more, have him working for his keep.

In response to Ernest's reply Isaiah began to make plans and his opportunity came a few days later when on one grey, damp morning a thoughtful

Peter Stiener saddled his horse and rode off without a word.

The likelihood was that Peter Stiener would not return for days and therefore Isaiah decided that he would leave at dawn the following day.

He cleared his room and then into saddle bags went the trappings of his independence; woollen socks and cardigan, linen shirts, cotton underwear, breeches, a spare pair of boots, oilskin cape, leather hat, pewter water bottle, carbolic soap, cutthroat razor, knife and sheath, leather-bound journal and graphite sticks, and a box containing the meagre savings he had managed to accumulate.

The short letter he then wrote to his father was poignant and not without bitterness. It read–

Dear Father,

By the time you read this I will no longer be a part of your life.

Our differences are totally irreconcilable, your God can never be my God, indeed no man's God can ever be my God.

For my entire adult life you have forced your will upon me with nothing but contempt for my feelings or beliefs.

Our relationship has been forged on nothing but altercation, violence and misery, and I end it here and now.

Goodbye, Father. I doubt that our paths will ever cross again.

In my thoughts I struggle to call myself your son.
Isaiah.

He then tucked the folded letter so that it protruded from under his academy Bible that Peter Stiener insisted should never be moved from a small oak bedside table.

3

At the hour before first light Isaiah saddled his big gelding, strapped on his saddlebags and after an anguished, prolonged farewell to his mother and Clara, he mounted the gelding and road off down the long tree-lined dirt road.

The overcast skies of previous days had cleared and he glanced back toward a flame-streaked eastern horizon and spurred the gelding into a cantor.

He breathed deep of the new morning air and exhilaration took him; then urging the gelding into a gallop laughed and then yelled the breath of freedom. His cry echoed back to the waving Ernestine and Clara, who were now tiny distant specks. Then, spurring the gelding onto the main coach road west, he rode on.

The coach road west cut through vast tracts of forest and sparse woodland that intermittently gave way to farmland and the occasional smallholding.

As dusk approached at the end of Isaiah's first day's ride, inevitable fatigue took him and he began to slouch in the saddle.

He scanned left and right into the deepening gloom through the great dark forest that stretched for miles either side of the road, and a momentary sense of desolation and loneliness shot through him.

Down a tiny track that veered off to the right he spotted a faint speck of orange light that glimmered in the distance through the trees, and seeking a night's rest, he spurred the gelding toward it.

That day he had ridden into a constant, sharp north-westerly breeze under a sky of fast-moving cloud that occasionally obliterated the sun, and by dusk the breeze had died and a chill mist appeared to drift upward through the trees. Isaiah shivered as a cold dampness slowly penetrated his woollen jacket.

After around a quarter of a mile he entered a clearing. A rambling cabin with outhouses had been built some distance from the track. Candlelight flickered through its one solitary window.

He dismounted and tapped on the door. After some time a woman, holding a club made from a whittled branch with a blood-stained wooden spike morticed into the top of the handle, half-opened the door.

The woman was a middle-aged hag, emaciated with long, dry matted ash-blonde/grey hair hanging to her chest. Her sunken cheeks were tawny-brown and her grey eyes were dark-rimmed and betrayed no shortage of suffering. She wore a filthy calico dress and black, scuffed mud-caked boots.

"What do ye want?" she drawled in a voice of whining tone.

"I mean you no harm, ma'am, I merely seek a resting place for the night, and perhaps some water for my horse."

The woman then opened the door wider, gripped the wooden club tighter and studied Isaiah for some time.

"Don't normally have a notion, considerin' possible danger of invitin' strangers inter ma cabin. Anyhow, havin' said that, of late ah don't much care whether ah live a die."

And with that she beckoned Isaiah in.

The cabin smelled of boiled nettles and forest mould. Numerous bunches of dried herbs hung from the walls and a half-skinned squirrel and a cleaver lay on a rough pine table.

"Ye can sit if ye wish," she said, as she poured him a beaker of nettle tea. "Aint got no vittles ter offer ye, that squirrel'll take tarm ter boil."

"That's no problem, ma'am, this tea is fine."

The tea tasted bitter, however it was warming and increased Isaiah's drowsiness.

"Ware ye travellin' ter, boy?" she said, at the same time as pouring herself some of the tea into an old dented tin mug.

"I am heading for St Louis," replied Isaiah.

"Ye got a heap o' miles ahead of ye. Ye can sleep in that hovel next ter ma pigsty. Ah will charge ye three dollars for the night."

The woman then studied Isaiah for a short while before a faint smile creased her lined cheeks.

"Aint had male company since ma Harky died, nigh on five year gone. If ye short of a dollar ye could perhaps pay me in kind," she said at the same time as raising her dress to reveal a scrawny varicosed calf.

"No, no ma'am, I have money," replied Isaiah, taken aback and recoiling.

"Well, ma'am, if it is alright with you, I am that tired, I am minded to turn in," Isaiah said, quickly draining his mug and backing toward the door.

"Soot yeself. Shack's on the right of the pigsty, can't miss it, smell'll most likely find ye first."

Isaiah watered his horse using an old bucket dipped into a brimming water barrel. He then tethered the gelding to a nearby tree and made his way to the shack next to the pigsty.

The door to the sty had rotted away from its hinges and it wedged and raked the ground as he pushed it open. The lightning dart of a rat across the scattered damp straw on the dirt floor startled him. In the dim light he could just make out the dark forms of stacked branches and twigs against the rear wall.

A number of the wooden boards that had originally panelled off the wall that divided the pigsty had either rotted or fallen away, and the entire shack stunk of stale swill and pig shit.

Finally, extreme weariness took him, and despite the rank odour, he lay down on the damp straw and fell into a deep slumber.

Isaiah woke to a grey dawn and the grunt and nuzzle of a lumbering sow. Although refreshed from a night's rest, he could taste pig odour and he briskly made his way to the water barrel, drank deep and plunged his head.

"Ma'am," he called, pushing open her cabin door.

The night candles were cold, and the woman was nowhere to be seen.

He left three dollars on the pine table, pulled the door shut, wrenched handfuls of twitch grass from the side of the cabin, fed them to his gelding, mounted and rode back down the track to the coach road and continued on westward.

A Park Drag and four thundered past him, churning mud up in the ruts as he cantered on.

After riding around twenty miles he reigned the

gelding in and dismounted in order to stretch his legs. Pig odour continued to taint his saliva and he cleared his throat and spat as he dismounted.

The realisation that he had been robbed struck him as he opened the leather flap of his saddlebag. In his weariness he had left the bags strapped to his gelding, and during the night the hag had helped herself. She had taken his spare woollen socks, his woollen cardigan and his carbolic soap.

He squatted by the side of the road, took a pull from his water bottle, and cursed himself for his lack of vigilance.

He then frantically checked his coat pockets and was relieved to discover that his journal and money remained safe.

Then after spending a few moments mulling over the events of the previous day, and feeling somewhat downcast, he remounted and rode on.

After his encounter with the hag, at night he slept in roadhouses, inns and settlements along the way, and there were times when he had little choice but to sleep rough where he could in wooded copses, fields or ditches.

It was dusk by the time he reached New Albany and after a day riding through saturating fine rain the yellow glow from the windows of the Pleasure Ridge Inn were a welcoming sight.

He rode into the forecourt, dismounted,

unstrapped his saddlebags, and handed the reins of the gelding to a bedraggled-looking stable hand.

The front door of the inn led to the main bar and wood panelled eating area. A number of travellers sat on worn wicker chairs at scrubbed timber tables eating. The roughly built bar was of heavy white oak and cigar and pipe smoke from a smattering of drinkers hung in the air and drifted blue across flickering oil lamps.

The fug of frying meat wafted through from the kitchen situated at the end of a short corridor at the rear.

A tall, bald, heavily perspiring man with side whiskers and drooping moustache, wearing a blood- and grease-stained apron appeared at the doorway; and without a word and stern-faced, the man gestured for Isaiah to sign the guest book, and then grabbing his saddlebags mumbled something about a single room and then beckoned him to follow.

He followed the man up a wide, creaking, polished stairway to a small attic room situated at the rear of the inn overlooking fields and distant woodland.

"No food after nine o'clock," the man muttered as he left the room and closed the door behind him.

The room was austere and smelled faintly of the frying that permeated from the kitchen below.

Under the window was a rough wooden bed with a straw palliasse. A terra cotta jug and bowl stood on a pine table by the left-hand wall. A hand-woven rug covered the polished floorboards.

After resting for a while on the Spartan bed Isaiah made his way back down to the bar where the innkeeper's daughter was serving drinks.

He caught her eye and her return glance betrayed an air of intrigue; and after taking his order for an evening meal she gestured for him to take a seat in the dining area.

The innkeeper's daughter was a young woman in her twenties. She would never have been thought of as pretty, however she was voluptuous and of sturdy build. Her arms were strong, her buttocks heavy, and her thighs powerful; the legacy of years of heavy work.

Her skin was pale and smooth with an alluring faint bloom.

She wore her ash-blonde hair in a top knot and her faded rose-patterned dress was buttoned to the neck and fastened with a tortoiseshell clasp.

Isaiah took his seat in the corner of the room and waited for his meal. By this time the bar had begun to fill with passing trade and the occasional staying guest.

In due course the innkeeper's daughter brought Isaiah his meal; slightly charred pork chops with boiled greens in a salty liquor, piled high and piping hot. The steaming dish was accompanied by a chunk of course bread and a tankard of beer.

Not having eaten for twelve hours Isaiah wolfed it down in ravenous fashion, finally mopping up the greens' liquor with the bread and washing the whole meal down with the warm, foaming beer.

Isaiah spent the remainder of the evening sitting at his table observing the activity at the bar and making entries in his leather-bound diary.

He studied the innkeeper's daughter with interest. He watched her flit from table to table, serve drinks and food, change barrels, share a joke with drinkers, and amid the general bustle of her work she would throw the occasional glance his way.

Towards the end of the evening, as the number of drinkers diminished, she found time to sit with him.

Her manner was quietly confident and unassuming. Her name was Rosheen and she was of Irish descent. Her mother had died of pneumonia, and she explained to Isaiah how she had felt duty-bound to replace her mother in assisting her father in the running of the inn.

She also told of how the inn had acquired its name. Her father had courted her mother at a lovers' haunt not far from the inn called Pleasure Ridge. When they were married and purchased the inn, they decided to name it after their old haunt.

Before drifting into a deep sleep that night, intermittent thoughts of Rosheen flashed through Isaiah's mind. Attracted to her he was, and spurred by anticipation he became minded to stay at the inn for longer than he originally intended.

And so the following morning he approached Rosheen's father and enquired as to the availability of his room for an extended stay.

"As long as you have the means to pay, sir, ye can stay as long as ye like," was his mildly gruff reply.

That evening Isaiah sat in his usual place and Rosheen served him his evening meal. The food was an improvement on the previous evening; again boiled greens, but this time with mutton stew. A large, elderly woman could be seen busy in the scullery area; the innkeeper was not the cook that evening.

After his meal Isaiah was in mellow mood. He sat observing the comings and goings at the inn and made more entries in his diary.

Later that evening a St Louis-bound coach pulled in for an overnight stop.

The clatter of shod hooves and the grind of steel rims on the forecourt interrupted the low murmur of voices at the bar. The rich odour of steaming horse dung drifted through an open window.

There were raised voices and intermittent laughter as the travellers climbed down onto the forecourt. Two identical cigar-smoking, grey-bearded men, dressed in beaver fur top hats, high-collared shirts, frock coats, breaches and riding boots strode through the door and up to the bar. A fine layer of road dust covered their shoulders. They were followed by three loud, giggling women, who flicked dust off their capes as they entered. A stable hand hefted valises and heavy trunks behind them. Then with characteristic lugubrious manner, and with as few words as possible, the innkeeper registered them in and showed them to their rooms.

Halfway through the evening, carrying an accordion, and accompanied by a fiddler and flute player, Rosheen's father walked into the bar, sat down on stools in front of the great fireplace and began playing the lilting folk songs of old Ireland.

Their initial playing was soft, slow and soulful and as the evening progressed the passion of their tunes increased in tempo and volume.

Perspiration poured off Rosheen's father's flushed brow as he stamped his feet to increasingly intoxicating rhythms. By ten o'clock the bar was heaving with drinkers all thoroughly enjoying the skilful musicianship.

Isaiah also became totally absorbed in the music and during a break in proceedings, in which the musicians downed dark beer from earthenware jugs, Isaiah approached the innkeeper, told him that he was in possession of a fair voice, and would be willing to sit in, in the final session. This then became a rare moment when the innkeeper forced a smile, and gestured for Isaiah to pull up a bar stool.

For the next hour, and accompanied by mournful playing, Isaiah sang the laments that Drummond had taught him; and his sweet tenor voice sent a hush amongst the previously noisy crowd, and Rosheen stood transfixed, and her intrigue for him gnawed deeper.

At the evening's end there were cheers for more, and with faintly moist eyes the innkeeper slapped the back of Isaiah and complimented him on stirring singing, and as the drinkers dispersed, went to their rooms or disappeared into the night, Isaiah was approached by the two cigar-smoking men who had arrived on the earlier St Louis bound coach.

The two men were identical twins and it was impossible to tell them apart.

"Ma name is Buller, Sir, Titus Buller, and this is ma brother Samuel. We are entrepreneurs."

The southern voice was high-pitched and both astringent and purposeful; characteristic of a man who was used to obtaining what he wanted.

He continued: "You have a very fine voice, sir. We are lookin' for a singer of your quality to perform on certain evenins in the saloon bar area of our boardin' house in St Louis. If, as ah presume, you are St Louis-bound, would you be interested in such an offer? We would of course provide accompaniment and pay you for your services."

Tainted with a slightly unsavoury air, Buller's manner belied his apparent pleasantness; however, Isaiah could not deny his interest. He intended to work purely for his keep at Ernest's store and his future would necessitate some means of income.

"I am pleased, sir, that you appreciate my singing.

"True I am headed for St Louis and I am tempted by your offer, and I will give it serious thought."

Then with fawning manner and a mildly insincere smile, he shook Isaiah's hand limply and concluded, "Our boardin' house is called Bullers and is located on the west side. I look forward to our reacquaintance in St Louis, mister..."

"Stiener, Isaiah Stiener."

Isaiah was blissfully ignorant of the fact that the Buller twins were unscrupulous fraudsters who had been involved in criminal activity for years. They had also gained a reputation for eliminating individuals who repeatedly failed to pay them the money they were owed, or reneged on a crooked deal.

They had dabbled in forgery, extortion and set up child prostitution rings, across a number of states, and whenever state law began to build up evidence against them, they repeatedly, through pure cunning, connived to remain one step ahead of the authorities, and then made a break for it with valises full of notes.

In the knowledge that St Louis was an expanding

boom town, and sensing opportunities for making large profits through gambling and liquor, they purchased a rundown hotel and converted it into Buller's boarding house and saloon, and even after Buller's had opened, the twins continued to lobby and blackmail financiers and politicians in Virginia in order to procure further investment in other possible St Louis-based rackets.

Isaiah returned to his room that night in satisfied mood and fell immediately into a contented sleep.

A gentle, incessant tapping on his door woke him around midnight.

He unlocked and opened the door; Rosheen stood there clad in nothing but a cotton nightshirt, the soft curves of her ample breasts visible through the light material. Her blonde hair hung low in cascades beyond her shoulders, and without a word she walked into the room and sat on the edge of the bed.

Pulse racing, Isaiah closed and locked the door behind her. Pale light through the window from the clear cloudless night touched her features and outlined the whiteness of her nightdress.

A curious, momentary flash of unreality seemed to check his consciousness as she stared up at him, lips parted, eyes wide and rolling, her black pupils dilated.

He breathed deeply as he ran his hand along her plump thigh. She quickly lifted and removed her nightgown. He caressed her hair and kissed her neck. She smelled of soap and oil of lavender. He buried his face into her cleavage and then licked her thick, erect nipples, and she whimpered with delight.

He ran his fingers through her pubic hair, and then lower into her private softness; and her moistness gushed onto his hand and then down onto her inner thigh.

Her kisses were powerful with her tongue searching oral depths. Rosheen broke off for a brief moment. Isaiah then stripped naked and again sat beside her. She produced a small bottle of almond oil from the pocket of her nightgown, removed the cork, poured some drops onto her palm and gently worked the oil onto his now glistening erection.

She then lay back, pulled up her knees, spread her thighs wide and coaxed him onto her. She panted as he entered her and gasped as he began to thrust with gentle rhythm. She raised her pelvis higher so that his penetration became deeper and then moaned softly into the darkness.

Isaiah's thrusting began to increase in intensity as he lost himself in the ecstasy of the moment.

Finally Rosheen groaned in her climax, clawing deep into him and drawing blood; and then with the searing delight of pain he ejaculated into her.

He continued to lay on her until his hardness died, and then he gently rolled over.

They lay together breathless in silence for some time until Rosheen jumped up, pulled on her nightgown, touched Isaiah's lips and quietly tiptoed back to her room.

After she had left he lay back, hands behind his head, deep in thought.

For some time she was still with him. He ran his tongue over his lips and tasted her. Her fading fragrance drifted from his chest, and the odour of her juices lingered on his loins; then as his pulse calmed a contented sleep took him.

Their lovemaking continued for a further three nights, however on the fourth morning Isaiah woke to an inner nagging voice of a restless nature. This pleasurable dalliance with an alluring woman could only ever be fleeting; his journey could not end here.

After breakfast he paid his dues to the innkeeper and Rosheen followed him to the stables where the gelding had been fed, watered and saddled.

Before mounting he pulled Rosheen to him.

For her, never was the ensuing embrace so poignant, never was an embrace so tinged with a longing so unrequited, and perhaps laced with a trace of a deeper, more profound intuition.

She stumbled over her words; they seemed disturbed.

"My life is here, in this place, I will always be here; perhaps ... perhaps another time."

She struggled to say more as he released his embrace. She stepped back and he mounted the gelding and then rode out onto the dirt road that led west.

She watched him ride away and slowly the increasing distance diminished her sight of him. He did not look back. On and on he rode until he finally vanished from view.

As he rode she returned to him again and again in his thoughts. He recalled the pleasure of their nights of intimacy, and could not deny a lingering desire for her; and repeatedly basked in the nostalgia of his brief time in her arms.

4

It was late evening when the oak door swung open and the great looming figure of Peter Stiener lumbered into the dimly lit hallway. His boots were caked with dried clay and grass, and his cape was mud-splattered. His face was flushed and an eight day growth bristled from his chin and cheeks. His bloodshot eyes were red rimmed and a white scum lined his lips.

A flickering orange line of light shone from under the parlour door where Ernestine and Clara sat in front of a roaring fire. Peter Stiener grunted and muttered to himself as he mounted the wide wooden stairs and made his way to his study.

The door to Isaiah's room was half open. Glancing into the room, even in the low light, he was struck by the room's unusual emptiness; it had been stripped of Isaiah's normal accoutrements and belongings. He walked into the room and pulled open the top drawer of an oak chest. Inside were piles of notebooks and drawing books of heavy grade cartridge. He flicked through the pages of one. Crude images of a strange subconscious nature reared up from its pages with an uncanny graphic force. Another book contained studies of Indian spiritual beliefs with marked references to the supposed power of a warrior's medicine bundle. In other drawers were boxes containing collections of small natural objects; the skull of a bird, a claw from a dead fox and small stones resembling figures were arranged in groups of six. The corner of a cream-coloured parchment peeped from under the dark bound Bible and it caught Peter Stiener's eye. He pushed the Bible back, grabbed the envelope and tore it open. He walked over to the light of the hallway and read his son's words; and with each word his fury simmered.

He then lumbered back down the creaking stairway and threw open the parlour door, knocking over a jardinière in the process.

"Explain this!" he rasped, throwing Isaiah's crumbled letter into the lap of Ernestine.

She was now staring straight into the fire and did not turn her head toward him.

"Isaiah's gone, left home for good," she said after scanning the letter.

"Are ye telling me that he has stolen away in my

absence, left home without a word, with scant and total disregard for me, after all that I have invested in him. And what is more abandoned his studies?"

His face and neck now pulsed with rage. Clara looked on cowering under his looming presence.

Ernestine now got up from her chair and faced him. In spite of her being small in stature she was a woman of forthright views and spoke her mind.

"You! You have driven our son away; he could not tolerate another day of your oppression and bullying. You have never allowed him the freedom to develop his own ideas. Why? Because they did not conform to yours, and you have forced him into a course of study that suited your needs and not his."

"That boy has denied God and is obsessed with Paganism," he roared. "No son of mine will treat me with disregard, nor will my word count for nothing."

Not for the first time Ernestine had got the better of her husband in altercation, and with each lash of her tongue, Peter's temper neared breaking point.

"You talk to me of God; you are nothing but a self-righteous prig. Your philandering is no secret to me. That boy is closer to God than you will ever be."

The blow to the side of Ernestine's head was executed like lightning. Peter Stiener's fist connected with Ernestine's temple in seconds, snapping her head sideways and knocking her back so that the base of her skull crashed against the heavy oak mantle. She then slumped to the hearth, her eyes rolling and her body convulsing; and then after a few seconds she lay still. The hem of her dress draped into the flames as she fell and it began to smoulder. Clara screamed, pulled her dress clear and stifled the burn. Clara shrieked again as she lifted Ernestine's head. Blood oozed from the back of her head onto Clara's hands. She listened to Ernestine's chest; there was no pulse and she did not breath.

The huge force of the blow to her temple had been instantly fatal.

"Dear God, you have killed her," Clara screamed, running her trembling hands over Ernestine's body and sobbing uncontrollably.

Peter Stiener began to back away toward the door, his face draining of colour with the sickening realisation that his impulsive blind rage, this time, had gone too far.

Then gripped by panic and guilt his only thought was to run. He clambered back up the stairs, opened his safe, filled a satchel with his savings, raced to the stables, saddled and mounted his mare and fled into the night, leaving a hysterical Clara numb with shock crouching over Ernestine's inert body.

Clara's world of contentment with her lifelong companion had been terminated in a matter of a few tragic moments. The speed at which her world had been turned on its head had left her in a temporary state of mental torpor in which rational thought was suspended and phases of disbelief were intermittently converted into shocks of reality.

After some time she became calmer, and even though Ernestine lay dead, she placed a cushion under the head of her oldest friend, closed the lids of her eyes and covered her body with a rug, and then only one thought reared in her mind; that of Bethany, Bethany, Bethany.

5

After a damp and cramped night in a ramshackled woodsman's hut, Isaiah woke to a dawn of chill mist. He drank from his water flask, watered the gelding, emptied his bladder on the ground, mounted his horse and rode on.

A yellow-grey light penetrated the spaces between the acid green spring foliage. After around a half of a mile woodland gave way to more open country, and as the sun rose the mist burned off, and the distant buildings of St Louis and the pale shimmer of the Mississippi were first visible on the grey-blue horizon.

The air became more oppressive as Isaiah entered the outskirts of the city after riding through the fresher air of forest and semi-marshland.

His thoughts simmered with anticipation at the prospect of a new life free from control and indoctrination. As he rode he recalled the dreary academy and of Armitage and Bowman and other members of his group, and became increasingly dumbfounded as to how young men of that ilk could opt so willingly for a life of restriction, and also be fed constant challengeable dogma.

He cantered down dirt roads, passed half-completed buildings, trudging passers-by and loaded carts pulled by mules, driven by dishevelled toil-worn men, toward the centre of the city.

The peeling sign, bolted to the front of a weatherboarded roof, read *Hackett's General Merchandise*. The store ran along a busy dirt road close to the centre of the city.

Ernest Hackett had established his business many years earlier at a time when St Louis was nothing more than a small expanding town. Within twenty years it would become a teeming city and the great natural gateway to the western frontier.

He had run his store with the help of his Mexican wife Morena, and the years had indeed seen them prosper; prosper enough to acquire land and build a large timber framed house with a veranda on the outskirts of the city.

It was around mid-morning when Isaiah climbed the boardwalk and entered the store. The odours of coffee beans, leather, iron, gun oil, molasses and resinous timber mingled in waves; and after serving two gaunt, bearded men in filthy clothes, Ernest and Morena subjected Isaiah to a pleasant, though less than emotional welcome. Both were stoical by nature, their lives had been hard and both were work-weary.

Ernest was short, balding, barrel-chested and heavily bearded. His hands were thick-fingered and calloused.

His wife Morena was taller, slender, with lined olive skin, and she appeared older than her forty years. Her thick wiry brown hair was shot through with grey. Her eyes were dark and her glance formidable. She had never suffered fools gladly and could be harsh if the mood took her.

After being greeted by Ernest and Morena, Isaiah became aware of a frail, slender figure standing in the doorway that led to the rear of the store. Smiling serenely and partially silhouetted by the light from a large rear window stood Isaiah's cousin Miguela.

Isaiah's memories of Miguela were as children before Ernest and Morena travelled to St Louis to establish their business. At that time Miguela had not been struck down by illness and his memories were of an extremely attractive child full of energy and kindness.

Illness took her before she reached her tenth birthday, and it was feared that she would not live.

Eventually, she was strong enough to make a

recovery, however disability and pulmonary weakness were to be the disease's legacy.

To enable her to walk her left leg required strapping in an iron and leather harness. The sole of her left boot had been made deeper to compensate for the difference in the length of her legs. She was exceptionally thin and sunken-chested as a result of the disease spreading to her lungs.

Her disabilities, however, were compensated by facial features of alluring beauty. Her pale skin was fine-grained, almost translucent. Her brown eyes were large, thick lashed and swept obliquely, almond-shaped, toward her temples; and her delicate nose led the eye down to full sumptuous lips. She wore her dark brown hair swept back, and then it hung in ringlets to her shoulders.

Her dress of deep red was trimmed with faded lace and around her neck hung a large crucifix of ivory. The apron she was wearing was soiled from the coffee she had been grinding.

Struck by her presence Isaiah walked over to her, took her hand and kissed her cheek.

"Wonderful to see you again, Isaiah, after so many years," she said, in a voice that was little more than a whisper.

In spite of her disabilities she had attracted the interest of a number of men, and had received proposals of marriage. None, however, had met with Ernest's approval; he was of the opinion that few men were worthy of her, and his protection of her was paramount. She was and remained the most precious thing in his life.

Morena and Miguela were both devout practising Catholics and they attended mass regularly and took holy communion. Indeed, so profound was Miguela's faith, and her devotion so absolute that she considered entering a convent. However, even the notion of her becoming a bride of Christ had not met with Ernest's approval.

That evening after the store was closed, they all rode to the Hackett's white-painted weatherboarded home on the edge of the city near scattered smallholdings and distant woodland, and they ate beef stew laced with chillies and pimentos, and they talked of family, of work, of God and of bygone years, and with each cup of wine Morena mellowed, and when all were drowsy from wine and work, Morena showed Isaiah to a small room at the rear of the house which would be his for as long as he wished to stay.

6

As a cool spring turned into warm early summer, and the evening light lengthened, Isaiah continued to work for his keep, lifting barrels, stacking shelves, loading and unloading wagons, and delivering supplies. And as time passed he developed a bond with Miguela. At Ernest's request Isaiah accompanied her whenever she ventured out, and they became close. They talked for hours, and as the weeks went by, her eyes brightened and she laughed more and more, and a new energy seemed to charge her struggling limbs, and each day Ernest beamed more with approval.

Trees thick with locusts lined the dirt road on which Buller's boarding house was located. Set back from the road, it consisted of two weatherboarded storeys, a ground floor saloon and rooms above.

It was late in the evening when Isaiah entered the saloon. A long bar ran down its entire length. At the far end was a raised dais and on it was an old battered upright piano.

A scattering of drinkers sat at tables playing cards. The Buller twins sat at a table at the far end deep in discussion with three other men. A veil of cigar smoke hung for a moment in the stale air above them, and drifted up to the tobacco-stained ceiling.

Isaiah walked over to the twins and stood apprehensively behind them, not knowing which one was Titus, the twin who had approached him at the Pleasure Ridge Inn.

Both men turned.

"Ah, Mister Stiener. Ah am pleased that you finally took the trouble to locate us," Titus said in a manner that implied that Isaiah had not responded to his offer with enough urgency, and without raising himself from his chair, and drawing on his thick cigar, he continued: "If it is acceptable to you, sir, we would be delighted if you could start performing tomorrow evenin', around eight o'clock. We will provide a pianist and two fiddlers, and we will pay you seven dollars per session with a possible increment to ten dependent on an increase in takins.'

This seemed reasonable to Isaiah and he nodded and both men shook hands.

The twins then turned their backs on Isaiah and resumed their discussions, and as Isaiah walked away he overheard Samuel mutter to the other man: "That boy can sing, ah am confident he will boost our profits."

And boost the Bullers' profits he did.

As the weeks went by word would spread of the fine singer performing at Buller's three evenings a week.

The Buller twins were delighted with the trade Isaiah's singing was pulling in. Sales in liquor and food exceeded their expectations, and true to their word they increased his session fee to ten dollars.

The shaky, drawling voice came from behind, at the end of one of Isaiah's evening performances. "Aint never heard a singin' voice like yourn afore, son. Tis without doubt very fine."

Isaiah turned. Standing there was an ageing frontiersman with loose, shoulder length white hair. He wore a soiled, double-breasted wool coat, frayed at the cuffs and a grubby high-collared calico shirt. His breeches were tucked into well-worn ex-army boots. His face was lined and weather-beaten, and around his neck hung an Indian amulet on a leather thong. He smelled of stale pee and whisky and he sucked on a long-stemmed clay pipe.

"With a sweet voice like that, stands ter reason ye should be performin' in them big Opry houses, not in this rough house of a drinkin' den. The name's

Wheber, H. Wheber," he said, extending a misshapen hand.

"My work here is only temporary," replied Isaiah. "However, I am grateful for your appreciation."

"Ware yer plannin' ter head next, son?"

"Well, sir, I feel deep the pull of freedom. I long to be away from the likes of this," nodding toward the mêlée of raucous, jabbering and laughing men. "I have a restless yearning to be away from teeming towns and cities. I am giving serious consideration to travelling west and maybe joining the fur trade."

Isaiah then paused and became thoughtful, and feeling mildly self-conscious under the old man's scrutiny he said, "I have deep issues within that I need to purge, and I feel that I may come to terms with them in a life in that beckoning wilderness."

Wheber looked quizzical and mildly surprised. He then drew on his pipe and stared at Isaiah for some time.

"Interestin' ye should say that, boy. Ye clearly have ye reasons. Used ter be a mountain man, worked for Hudson's Bay. Trapped with the likes of Joe Meeker and Josh Rimmer. Came back in twenty five; arthritis did for me."

He held up two gnarled and twisted hands.

"The life's infernal hard, thar aint much money in it, and thar's danger, danger at every turn, night 'n day."

Lifting a nobbled hand he swept the long white hair from the left side of his face to reveal a puckered hole that now serviced as an ear. The channel of an ugly scar ran from the hole down his neck to his shoulder.

"Arikara Hawk – Tomahawk, took off ma whole fuckin' ear."

His expression clouded slightly with tension at the recall.

"Thar's a damn good chance'a you losin' yer hair. Anyhow, if'ern that's the track ye minded ter take, boy, best follow yer instincts.

"Speakin' of Josh Rimmer, ah heard a rumour that he's here in St Louis, and coincidentally ah heard that he's lookin' ter go cahoots with somebody strong and willin'. By all accounts he's aimin' ter increase his pew tally, make a last killin' while thar's still life in the fur trade afore he retires with his squaw ter his adobe in Taos." And then sucking on his pipe and sizing Isaiah up he said, "Coincidentally, boy, yer look like yer might fit his bill."

"Where might I find this Rimmer?"

"Thar's a chance he'll be at Creed's. It's a shack of a drinkin' hole on the edge of town, due west of here."

He then paused. "Havin' said that, for all ah know he may have found a partner and he's now long gone; struck back up the Missouri. Ye takes ye chances, boy. Ah wish ye good fortune, boy," Wheber finally said as he turned away and then he turned again whilst shuffling back to the bar. "A word of warnin'. Them 'as cross Josh Rimmer do not normally live ter tell the tale. He's a killer and ruthless, but he's fair and he's a man of his word."

7

> Until I tread where you tread, clutch at your power and feel your senses. Only then can I face the wind.
> – Thoughts of a holy man.

Creed's Tavern lay off the main dirt road that led into the city from a westerly direction. It was surrounded by scrubland and clumps of trees. It was no more than a large log and mud-caulked cabin with a packed dirt floor.

On the mud-churned land at the rear was a ramshackled chicken coup and a pigsty. Empty barrels and logs were piled high against the rear wall. A black, half-starved mongrel was chained to a post amid gnawed bones and shitpiles, and it yapped and growled at every passer-by.

It was the hour before dusk when Isaiah strode into its gloomy interior. A crude bar ran along a section of the right-hand wall. Behind the bar was a row of tapped barrels resting on wooden cross frames. At one end was an iron log-fired stove with a tin smoke flue that ran up through the roof. On the stove were pots of bubbling coffee. Elk horns and frontier relics adorned the walls. Heavily bearded, wild-haired men drank, smoked and muttered in low voices at trestle bench tables. The atmosphere was thick with tobacco smoke and fumes from cheap tallow candles wedged into bottles.

The barkeep was a hulk of a man with a shaved head and a long beard that hung in braided strands.

Isaiah ordered a small beer and enquired as to the whereabouts of a Mister Rimmer. The barkeep nodded towards the far end of the tavern.

Amid the fug of pipe smoke and the general gloom, a figure sat with its back to the log wall. A tallowed line of light touched the left side of the figure highlighting a slightly foreboding presence.

Josh Rimmer was now fifty-eight years old. His dark, lined and crease-riven features were clean shaven. Age stains and the occasional benign tumour sprinkled his temples. His grey hair hung almost to his waist. Beads had been woven into the right-side of his scalp lock, and around his neck hung a necklace of bear claws. Both ears had been pierced with thick silver rings, and yellow eyes cut like lances to the viscera.

His fringed buckskins shone black with grease and his moccasins of thick rawhide were bound and laced to the knee. A maple-handled seven inch long hunter Green River in a tooled leather sheath hung from his left hip. He smelled of tobacco and ageing leather and about him was a faint elusive aura of the wilderness.

For years he had been employed by the Hudson's Bay Company working with bands of mountain men on numerous trapping expeditions. Unlike most of his breed, who frittered away their earnings on drink and women, he had been frugal, managing to save enough to build a small adobe on the outskirts of Taos, and it was here that he intended to spend his final years.

As the fur trade boomed he quit Hudson's Bay and became a free trapper working alone or with a partner.

Now at fifty-eight years old there were signs of rheumatism in his joints, and his days as a mountain man, he considered, were probably numbered, and again it was a partner he now sought.

As Isaiah walked toward the shadowy figure, beer tankard in hand, he came to the sudden conclusion that it would be best to approach

Rimmer in a forthright manner. However, his immediate delivery turned out to be embarrassingly obsequious.

"Good evening t'you, sir," he said. "My name is Isaiah Stiener. I have been informed by a Mister Wheber, with whom I believe you are acquainted, that you have been on the look-out for a partner. I do possess the strength and will for any work. Perhaps you could be minded to give me some consideration, sir."

Rimmer did not reply. He drew deeply on his pipe, exhaled a cloud of tobacco smoke and studied Isaiah for some time. Isaiah continued to stand in front of him feeling foolish.

Rimmer looked favourably at what stood before him. Here was a tall youth of powerful build with a facial expression that indicated a cool disposition.

He finally broke his silence.

"How old are ye, boy?"

His voice was rasping and seemed to emanate from deep in his throat.

"I am nineteen years old, sir."

"More'an likely git yerself kilt in them mountains. Thar's a chance ye mayn't see twenty."

He then nodded toward a stool for Isaiah to sit and beckoned the barkeep to recharge his mug of coffee and top up Isaiah's beer. They both sat in silence once again while Rimmer drew repeatedly on his pipe and sipped his coffee.

"Ever see a red coon in full war regalia afore, boy?"

"No, sir."

"If them coons don't rub ye out, the elements might. Life's infernal hard in them mountains and plains; could git froze ter death in them high passes in a norther or at best frostbit. A dust storm on the plains could take ye skin off or blind ye; ye'll be wadin' for hours up ter yer knees in icy water layin' traps in a cold mist. Thar are times when it rains for days, turnin' tracks inter mud flats. Summer heat's so damn fierce as ter cut ye down, and if ye don't know ware ter find water ye finished."

He then took another draw and continued.

"Heerd at last Rendivoo Elbridge Hands got rubbed out up in the San Juans; party o' Utes ambushed 'im and 'is squaw just afore they broke camp.

"Old Elbridge was a fine Hiverano, well up ter the Beaver. Heerd tell that the Utes had a score ter settle with 'im. Damn fool offloaded some bad wheat liquor to 'em in a trade. Sent some of 'em in ter demented fits; two of 'em went blind through drinkin' too much o' the stuff.

"Ute Shaman figured it was some kind o' demon potion that called down bad spirits. Shaman tried all kinds o' spells and hokum ter drive out them spirits. Did no good, more of 'em went blind."

At this point Isaiah began to doubt the credence

of Rimmer's ramblings and was struck by a sudden wave of apprehension.

Rimmer then paused, took a mouthful of coffee and continued.

"Anyhow, the Utes finally sent out a party to track Elbridge down and take revenge. They found 'im and 'is squaw camped on the Animas.

"Them Utes took revenge and some. Elbridge was found with twenty arrows in 'im, most of 'em in 'is eyes, head and neck. His squaw took almost as many. By all accounts he took five of 'em with 'im before they cut 'im down. His squaw put up some fight too. She gutted two of 'em before they raped her and used her belly and tits fer targit practice. Them Utes didn't care; she was uglier 'an a mule's balls, and still they raped her raw.

"Like I said, thar's a fair chance o' dyin' in them mountains."

Then again, after what seemed another interminable silence in which Rimmer appeared to cogitate and with a final deep draw on his pipe he said, "Ye got somethin' about ye, boy, and ah am minded ter go cahoots with ye. I'll expect ye here tomorrow around two hours afore sundown."

After which he said no more, rose from his chair, threw some coins on the table, and with purposeful smooth, rolling strides, made his way out of the tavern, mounted his mule and rode off.

The following late afternoon, from Creed's

Tavern, with Rimmer's mule dwarfed by Isaiah's big gelding, they backtracked through city alleyways to head north-west toward semi-marshland and the river.

Isaiah was clueless as to where they were headed with Rimmer talking incessantly as they rode.

"Yer need backbone, boy," he said. "Life in them mountains is life on a knife edge; requires instincts and senses beyond them of ordinary men," and he continued to mutter about the vastness and magnitude of the land beyond the Missouri, and a life of freedom where a man is answerable to no one but himself, and Isaiah could not deny the power of his words.

They reached alleyways too narrow to ride through, so they dismounted and walked their mounts.

The late spring evening was uncharacteristically sultry, with swarms of midges hanging in the air. They passed looming weatherboarded warehouses and rough timber shacks. A fly-infested dead dog lay by the side of a wall.

As they walked on a young girl ran from the doorway of a dark shack of a bordello and blocked Isaiah's way. She lifted her skirts to reveal pale slender thighs and a thick triangle of pubic hair. She ran her fingers downward toward her groin.

"This could be yours, young sir. Only a few

dollars. Show yer a good time," she cackled. "Only a few dollars."

Isaiah stood momentarily transfixed until Rimmer pushed him on.

"Don't touch 'em, boy. Most of 'em are clap- or pox-ridden. And what's more yer payin' fer a possible goddamn dose. Git yourself an Indian woman. Thar pretty much clean."

As they walked on Isaiah glanced back and as he did so the girl called, "Don't know what yer missin'," running her fingers through her ample pubic tufts.

They walked on and turned into a dark alley where shadows patterned the ground. The narrow walkway was barely wide enough for man or horse.

Two men dressed in dark city clothes cut into the alley some distance away and slowly approached from the opposite direction. They came to a halt in front of Rimmer. One was tall, well over six feet, the other shorter and of more stocky build.

"Make way there," barked the taller man.

Rimmer immediately adopted an air of defiance and stood his ground.

A subtle odour of brothel-tainted cologne, tobacco and sweat emanated from both men.

"What have we here? A breed, and maybe a squaw lover at that. Have respect for white men and step aside."

Rimmer continued to stand his ground motionless and stare out his man.

Anger flared in the tall man's nostrils as he repeated, "Step aside you breed scum. I don't believe you heard me the first time."

"I heard ye the first time," replied Rimmer, his voice calm and low.

"Well I beg to differ. It is my opinion that you really don't hear so good," said the tall man, at the same time pulling a Bowie knife from beneath his long dusty grey linen jacket.

The man then edged closer in an attempt to face Rimmer down and began to toss his knife from hand to hand in a foolish attempt to mesmerise, finally making a clumsy lunge toward Rimmer's ribs.

A rapid sequence of sense-defying movements then took the moment as Rimmer's Green River appeared in his right hand and with a twist of the body and a sudden lurch sideways he parried the lunge and the man's blade thrashed air. Rimmer's blade then appeared driven to the hilt in the man's abdomen, and then upward it lacerated to the base of the sternum, and then it pulled clear.

The tall man's eyes began to cloud with disbelief, shock and then fear as he dropped his knife and sank to his knees. Blood and intestinal fluid saturated his breeches as he attempted to hold the slit of the wound together, and then the air suddenly became fowl with the stench of his evacuating bowels as he rolled onto his side.

Meanwhile, the shorter man, with fists flaying,

made a dive at Isaiah, but to no avail. Isaiah heaved him away so that he staggered back, stumbled to the ground, and then glancing at the bloody mess Rimmer had made of his companion, he got to his feet and tore back down the alley from whence he had come.

"I aint no breed, I'm as white as you," Rimmer said as he wiped the blade of his Green River on the tall man's shoulder and resheathed.

The man gazed up at him with eyes wet with tears. His mouth gaped and the scream that should have come became stifled by a gurgling surge of blood.

"He was a damn fool, knife-fightin' is just ma game. He'll take a while ter die," Rimmer rasped, and as they walked on Isaiah endeavoured to suppress any outward sign of revulsion. However, his stomach had churned at the sight of Rimmer's bloody butchery and he was minded starkly of Wheber's parting words.

After clearing the narrow alleys on foot they remounted and rode on. Gradually the oppressive atmosphere of the city began to give way to the fresher air of more open country. They passed scattered smallholdings and cottonwood copses. An old man sitting outside a cabin waved at Rimmer as he passed, and Rimmer touched his forehead in response. After a while they entered thicker stretches of woodland. Glints of crimson from the setting sun flashed through gaps in the trees. Finally, they emerged in a secluded, almost hidden grove.

The odour of woodsmoke filled the breezeless spring air. Hides had been thrown over the lower branches of a tree near the bank of a stream to make a temporary tipi.

An Indian woman crouched over a bubbling cast iron kettle. As Isaiah and Rimmer dismounted, the woman rose from the fire and came to greet them. She was tall and graceful, unlike many Indian women who were squat in stature, flat-faced and narrow-eyed.

"This is ma woman," Rimmer said. "She's Crow, she's called Watseka."

Watseka had been with Rimmer for a number of years. She had been a real beauty in her youth and Rimmer had paid her father a generous purse for her hand. She was now in her twenty-ninth year, almost thirty years Rimmer's junior, and still handsome.

Premature grey streaks highlighted her thick black calf-length hair. She was unusually light-skinned for an Indian woman; fine and honey-toned, it appeared delicately lustrous in the evening light. She wore a gold ring in each ear, and from each hung tiny white bones.

Isaiah extended his hand as she approached, but she smiled and backed away. The gentle quiver of her fine buttocks through her doeskin skirt caught his eye as she turned and entered the makeshift shelter. She spread blankets around the fire; Rimmer and Isaiah sat cross-legged and with smooth lilting grace Watseka dished up the bubbling fare onto tin plates. It smelled of fat, of the earth and of boiled blood, and Rimmer spooned it down in ravenous fashion.

The flicker of flames, the soporific fading light of a sultry dusk, and Watseka's shaded presence were mesmeric, and Isaiah became absorbed by a strange trance of calm.

He knew not what had boiled in the pot, however he found the meat sweet and tender. It floated in a fatty simmering broth of ambiguous strange flavour that yet seemed to evoke a sense of the land, of wild grasses, and rain born on the wind.

After they had eaten Watseka gathered the empty tin plates and Rimmer lent back and lit his pipe. Transfixed by her every movement, Isaiah thought her magnificent as the glow from the fire touched her features and the flames danced in her wide black eyes.

Indeed, so transfixed was he that at one point he forced himself to avert his gaze, respectful of the fact that she was Rimmer's woman. Rimmer, however, appeared oblivious, and in relaxed mood, gazing into the fire whilst he drew on his pipe.

She spoke to Rimmer in Crow in a lilting, low

voice that rippled through the still air; here was a woman born of a primal land, a land beyond time.

After a while Rimmer began to drawl on and on and lit pipe after pipe until night fell and the embers began to die, and Isaiah sat and listened.

That night, laying on a buffalo robe under the seclusion of overhanging branches, sleep evaded him for some time. Rimmer and Watseka lay together under the makeshift tipi.

The challenges that lay ahead and the allure of an unreachable woman churned constantly in his thoughts.

The black night glittered and was silent save Rimmer's low snoring, the crackle of fading embers, and the ripple of the stream. A beast howled in the unknown distance and eventually sleep took him.

The silence of the hour before dawn, when Isaiah woke, was broken by the sound of Rimmer grunting as he urinated into the stream. Watseka had managed to breathe life into the fire, and the quiver of her breasts beneath her doeskin dress did not escape Isaiah's eye, as she raked the embers with a branch.

They sat and drank coffee as the sun rose and Rimmer lit his first pipe of the day.

After Watseka had shaved him, he brought out his rifle and proceeded to emphasise its qualities to a fascinated Isaiah.

Rimmer's Hawken rifle was a special piece;

cleaned, oiled and cared for down the years, it was without doubt a thing of beauty. Weighing ten and three quarter pounds, it was an old model fifty four caliber Plains rifle. The polished stock of maple had a rich honey-red lustre, with rippling grain. The inlaid furniture and curved butt plate were of bright iron, and the triggers were double-set with a scroll iron guard; and the octagonal barrel glinted grey-blue in the firelight.

"Like a woman's thigh," Rimmer muttered, as he stroked the smooth maple stock, and at the same time glancing up at Watseka.

Isaiah took the rifle, touched its fine finish, pulled it to his shoulder, felt the perfect weight and balance, sighted down the barrel and sensed the soul of the piece; sensed its brutal past and the lives it had taken.

To Rimmer the Hawken rifle and the Green River were visceral to any trapper worth their salt and he would not even consider going cahoots with a young protégé without him acquiring both, so that morning they rode to Jacob and Sam Hawken's gun shop in St Louis.

They retraced their steps back into the city; through the narrow alley where Rimmer had killed the knife-wielding man. There was no sign of his body, only a dark stain in the packed dirt path remained. They passed the dark shack of a brothel where the young whore had revealed herself.

"Whore still on ye mind, boy?" Rimmer said, noticing a vaguely pensive look in Isaiah's eyes as they passed. "Like ah said, them whores is best left be."

The young whore, however, could not have been further from his desires; it was Watseka who continued to dog his thoughts with a hopeless yearning.

At Hawken's, after settling a price with Jacob Hawken for a fine reconditioned piece with which Isaiah was more than enamoured, Rimmer perused the shop, and in a cabinet under glass lay a weapon of intrigue. The Collier was a revolver, a pistol with a manually revolving chamber enabling five shots to be fired without reloading. Rimmer was drawn to it, handled it, tested its action. It proved awkward, poorly balanced, yet he saw in it a piece that, provided it did not misfire, could give him an edge in a fight. Newfangled as it was, surprisingly Rimmer fell for it and the gun became his at a fair price.

As they rode away from Hawken's Rimmer drawled on.

"Now listen ter me, boy. The riverboat leaves for Leavenworth and Fort Pierre in four days. It is ma intention that we be on that steamboat in good time; be at ma camp in two days. We'll break camp the followin' mornin' and then make our way up river to the wharves whar she's moored."

"I will not let you down, sir. I will be there," replied Isaiah.

"You will have time to make yer goodbyes and pack yer essentials. We have a journey of over a thousand miles ahead of us. We're bound for Absaroka, Crow land; ah am on good terms with the Crow. Ah have a cabin that ah use as a trappin' base 'bout twenty or so mile from Watseka's relatives' winter village.

"We should reach ma cabin around October. It is ma intention that we winter thar and prepare for spring trappin', that's when beaver plews is prime. Trap in the Buck Moon and ye'll git poor plews. Rendivoo'll be at Green River, Wyomin'.

"In case ye wondrin', boy, Rendivoo is a gatherin' like no other."

Rimmer's tone then became mildly introspective. Rimmer had a way with him, a way with words that at times dove deep; a way of riveting whoever listened. In his crude mountain way he could be compelling. He continued almost lyrically and his words were never wasted on Isaiah.

"They'll come, they'll come from afar, from Yellowstone and the Bighorns, from the Black Hills and the Medicine Bow, from Clearwater and the Bitterroots.

"They'll come mostly ter trade, gamble, fight, git assholed on Tangle Foot, and fornicate with as many coon women as they can lay thar hands on.

"It'll last for days and the livin'll be wild, and then they'll disperse. Some'll be back followin' year, and some ye'll never set eyes on agin."

Rimmer turned as he rode away. "And one other thing, boy. Leave that big geldin' of yourn behind. He aint nimble enough for ware we're headed."

There was much consternation, disappointment and sadness at Isaiah's impending departure, none more so than from Miguela, the bond between them having grown stronger each day. Periods of happiness in Miguela's life had been sporadic and brief, and likewise Isaiah's sojourn with her had been all too fleeting. He had become a beacon of light in what had been an unfortunate life dogged by ill-health.

Ernest made it known that he would miss Isaiah's manpower, however he accepted his desire to leave and said a reluctant goodbye. Morena on the other hand became openly tetchy and made disappointing remarks to the effect that she and Ernest had taken the trouble to oblige Isaiah with food and keep and now, after such a short period, he was deserting them.

Before he left he embraced Miguela's spare, delicate body, stroked her hair, felt the sharpness of her shoulder blades, and ran his hands down to her tiny waist, and felt helpless in her sorrow at his leaving.

He made a gift of his horse to her and informed her that perhaps one day he would return.

The Buller twins were not best pleased when Isaiah informed them of his intentions. Both Titus and Samuel displayed an unpleasant, truculent side to their character at the prospect of one of their main profit-generating assets leaving.

They berated Isaiah for not giving them due notice; they became threatening and informed him in no uncertain terms that all monies owed to him would now not be paid. They had never, however, been prompt payers and were in fact three performances in arrears.

Isaiah took without reply their verbal tirade and in the assumption that he would never cross their paths again he turned, and without a word walked briskly out of the Buller's boarding house and headed for Rimmer's camp.

He had sensed the stalker for some time before turning quickly. A tall, hulking figure appeared to cut back into the shadows.

Isaiah walked on and turned again; this time there was no one there, however he continued to sense a lurking presence. Isaiah walked on briskly and cut into the alley where Rimmer had done his worst, finally arriving at the brothel. A dark slit of a passage ran down the side of the brothel. Isaiah squeezed himself into it and waited. The young blonde whore leant from one of the first floor windows, her breasts flashing white, ready for business.

The dark, hulking figure finally appeared, trudging slowly with a lurching tread, flashing eyes scanning right and left. Greasy, matted black hair hung over the shoulders of a filthy grey linen coat. The outline of a cudgel hanging from a belt loop was just visible as his unbuttoned coat swayed.

He turned and entered the brothel; the unwashed odour of festering body fluids wafted into the narrow gap in which Isaiah hid. He recognised the man, he had seen him before, on certain nights at Buller's saloon. A sinister, repulsive presence, always sitting alone, always in the shadows.

After what seemed an age the man reappeared and trudged on his way with the same loping tread until out of sight.

Isaiah finally emerged from the tiny passage and crossed the walkway.

"You again, young sir. Why not spend some time with me? Come on, young sir."

The whore's voice rang clear.

Isaiah glanced up and caught sight of the creamy white of her breasts.

Within seconds she appeared in the shadow of the doorway and beckoned to him.

She looked alluring in the dim light, and wary of the stalker doubling back, he succumbed to temptation and walked over to her. Up close her pretty face appeared heavily painted. Her eyes were black with crude shadow and the cheap perfume she wore was tainted with pungent body odour. An old scar that cut through her eyebrow had the effect of distorting her right eye. Her smile revealed decay-ravaged teeth and her sour breath caught Isaiah's nostrils as she pulled him into a dark corridor and guided his hand to the soft flesh of her inner thighs. Desire then took him as she ran her fingers over his ample hardness.

"This is a prize indeed," she whispered, at the same time pulling him into a dingy, rough panelled passage that led to crude stairs.

He followed her up the stairs and then along another dark corridor.

Through an open door two heavy-set, bearded men sat playing cards in a candlelit room. Primed pistols and wooden cudgels hung on racks on the rough planked walls. Sudden apprehension gripped him; had he been a fool to allow his loins to rule his head? Rimmer had been right. Whores were best left alone. Compulsion, however, won the moment and Isaiah followed the girl into a small room, and slamming the door behind her, the young prostitute stripped herself naked in a matter of seconds.

Isaiah sat on the edge of a rough pine-framed bed that was positioned in the centre of the room. The girl was tall and slender with pale skin prone to blushing at the neck and upper arms. She possessed fine, gentle curves with breasts that were small but pert. Her mulberry-coloured nipples stood firm and erect.

"C'mon then, get them breeches off," she said, flashing her ugly teeth in a broad smile.

Isaiah unbuttoned them, slid them down and lay back on the bed.

The girl then knelt beside him and began to gently pump his erection.

She pushed him away when he attempted to pull her to him saying, "No huggy-huggy".

She then deftly applied a sheep's bladder to his penis, straddled him and lowered herself onto his hardness.

She proved skilled in the manipulation of her vaginal muscles with the rise and fall of her hips and buttocks to create sensations that were excruciating, and sent Isaiah into a short burst of ecstasy that lasted but for a few seconds. She then felt the throb of his ejaculation and suddenly pulled herself clear, leaving Isaiah feeling mildly foolish.

"Well, that was short 'n' sweet, young sir. Never the time of yer life though. That'll be fifteen dollars. Call again!"

Isaiah left the brothel feeling downcast, and making his way down the tracks that led out of the city he cursed himself for allowing his loins to rule his head, and what was more, ending up fifteen dollars to the worse, all for a few seconds of high sensation.

Retracing the route he had walked with Rimmer he finally broke out into more open country and recognised the familiar smallholdings.

It was dusk when he entered the clumps of woodland, and as darkness fell his sense of direction began to fail with each copse and clearing appearing like any other.

Eventually he found himself wandering aimlessly through the near black night, and realising he had become lost, anxiety gripped him.

The rustle in the trees came from behind; thoughts of the stalker flashed through his mind as he whipped round and levelled the Hawken. A figure shrouded in faint light emerged through the undergrowth.

The figure threw up its arms as the click of the hammer broke the silence of the night. The figure called to him in a voice that was almost a whisper. It was a woman's voice. It was the voice of Watseka. She beckoned to him and gestured back the way she had come. He followed her for at least a quarter of a mile until the flicker of low flames appeared through gaps in the foliage. They finally cut through into the secluded grove.

Rimmer lay against a rolled blanket smoking his pipe and sipping from a mug of coffee.

"She sensed ye comin', boy," he drawled. "Figured ye were wandrin' lost."

Isaiah walked over to the fire, dumped his bag,

propped his Hawken, shook Rimmer's hand, and felt foolish for the second time that day.

They ate fried crayfish and drank coffee, and Rimmer lit pipe after pipe and rambled on and on mainly about past skirmishes with 'real coons' and white men alike.

Watseka sat in silence, cross-legged whittling what appeared to be the crude form of a bird.

Isaiah woke at dawn to the sound of Watseka breaking camp and loading the mule.

Rimmer stood naked in the stream cupping water over his lean body. He then shaved with the aid of what appeared to be an ancient tarnished wood-framed mirror wedged in the V of a branch.

8

After downing a pot of coffee and dousing the campfire, they set off, making their way north, through scattered copse and semi-marshland, toward the St Louis wharves. Isaiah and Rimmer walked behind Watseka who rode the mule; her hair swaying across her shoulders with the mule's lope, and glinting in the morning sunlight.

Rimmer remained perpetually expressionless, his face never betraying any emotion. His expression lightened only when he was amused or was being magnanimous regarding an act of violence.

After around three miles the land widened and they reached the shoreline washed by the confluence of the great Missouri and Mississippi rivers. The Floridiana steamboat was a new large, two-funnelled vessel with two decks. She was moored to a wide-planked jetty that thrust out from the St Louis wharves. She was due to cast off at noon that day and she was a hive of activity. A procession of trappers, hunters, men in uniform bound for Leavenworth and a group of missionaries all boarded her and paid their dues to the quartermaster. Cargo and livestock were being herded and loaded onto the lower deck.

While Watseka offloaded the mule, Isaiah and Rimmer paid their passage and carried their possibles and accoutrements on board. Watseka led the mule down to the lower deck.

At the stern of the vessel groups of men sat around talking and smoking, waiting for cast off. Amongst the trappers Rimmer acknowledged one or two familiar faces from past Rendezvous and immediately struck up conversation.

Watseka sat quietly and continued whittling her tiny wooden totem.

At noon, with a blast on its siren and to a peel of cheers, the Floridiana cast off and moved slowly into the great expanse of the river to begin its journey west. The missionaries formed a circle on deck and began a prayer meeting, finishing off with a droning verse of *Lead Kindly Light*.

Rimmer turned to Isaiah: "Ah don't hold with them God lovers tryin' ter convert all 'n' sundry ter thar persuasion. Red coons got thar own beliefs, have had for nigh on a thousand year. Leave 'em be, that's what ah say.

"Whar thar headin' thar hair'll more'an likely end up as a trophy on a lance, that's just about as far as prayin'll get 'em."

The following morning, after a restless night on a robe on the hard deck, Isaiah woke at dawn. The weather had remained calm with a hint of breeze. He stood by the handrail of the boat and drank in the scene before him. The great cloudless sky seemed to envelope the wide murmuring river as the steamer surged forward, and an adrenalin of anticipation coursed through him. However, this euphoria, born of thoughts of adventure that may lay in store in the weeks and months ahead, was tempered by an occasional low undertone of foreboding.

As the days turned into weeks and the steamboat ate up the miles and made its way through the upper Missouri, the landscape gradually transformed.

With the primordial greatness of the land and the breath-taking infinity of expanse and distance, spiritual notions that had hitherto been anathema to him, began to change Isaiah's thoughts. Beyond the reach of his city-generated notions and ideas, here was a dimension of beauty that sublimated emotions and imagination. If God did dwell anywhere other than in the minds of men then surely it would be here.

The steamboat cut through great swathes of rich forest of Aspen, Juniper, and Grey Elder, only then to break into restful rolling flat land; and then again be enveloped by inspiring walls of creviced sandstone, reaching to eye-watering heights, to touch the great cupola of sky.

Occasionally in small clearings dark-skinned figures would appear, and once Isaiah caught sight of the tiny transient figure of an Indian girl emerging from a black forest hole, the sunlight glinting on her deerskin dress; her black hair and the beadwork of her moccasins appearing to shimmer in the hazy distance. And then she was gone, and her absence left him with a yearning for her to return. And all the while the great purple and white cyclorama of the mountains would intermittently appear in the untouchable distance.

Throughout the river journey Watseka remained quiet. When she was not whittling her small totem she sat staring out toward the land, her verbal communications with Rimmer being few and far between.

Emerging from her whittling was what appeared to be the form of a wingless bird. During the long hours of tedium on deck Isaiah made entries in his diary, and also from time to time found himself distracted and intermittently observing the stoical Watseka, and this did not escape Rimmer's eyes.

"Wondrin' what that's all about, boy?" he grunted.

Isaiah gave a mildly self-conscious nod, again being inwardly wary of his occasional perusal of Rimmer's woman.

As was his way, before Rimmer embarked on any kind of description or tale, there was a long lugubrious pause while he drew on his pipe and cogitated, then he would eventually begin.

"When she was young Watseka was dogged by a nightmare of a great hawk. Them earrings o' hers are hawk bones. Crow Shaman figured the hawk was a messenger from the spirit world, so he moaned some kind o' hokum through fire 'n' smoke ter send the hawk back never ter return. Then, thereafter, low 'n' behold her visions began ter fade and the Shaman appeared ter have done his work."

Rimmer then took his usual pause in order to draw once more on his pipe and then continued.

"Now here's a thing. Some nights past, the hawk came back again in a dream. This time it was bigger'an a she-wolf, and it appeared ter be clutchin' somethin' in its claws. It then flew away, disappearin' inter distance. It weren't clear what the hawk was carryin', and ever since the vision has worried her. Crows believe that objects linked ter dreams and visions are sacred. The Shaman will weave his hokum over that carving ter send that spirit hawk back once and fer all. Stands to reason, aint no way a wingless hawk could fly back.

"Ter me it's all hogwash, anyhow. Ah have some respect for Watseka's beliefs.

Watseka had turned and sat deep in thought, gazing out toward the gradually changing shoreline, and her silent presence became even more compelling.

Delattre was a Breton, a murderer and a rapist. He had come to the mountains in order to flee French justice. He had been a free trapper for a number of years, however this year of 1830 he had enlisted with The Rocky Mountain Fur Company and was now on his way to Leavenworth to join a recruited band of fur company trappers.

He had had a succession of Indian wives, all of whom had met a brutal end at his hands. Thick set, heavily bearded, and shaven-headed, he was arrogant and cruel, and would not hesitate to kill to achieve his ends. He possessed an insatiable appetite for Indian women and inevitably the sultry Watseka had caught his eye.

One evening after a heavy fill of Tangle Foot he made his move. He had had past dealings with bands of Crow and had acquired a smattering of their language, and squatting next to Watseka he began an attempt to seduce her, muttering in a low voice, punctuated with short bursts of chuckling.

Watseka remained oblivious to him and continued to whittle.

Delattre persisted, and eventually becoming irritated with Watseka's refusal to respond, he placed his arm on her shoulder and attempted to pull her to him. Watseka recoiled at this and barked a rebuff.

None of this went unnoticed by Rimmer who was sitting with Isaiah and a small group of men some distance away.

Rimmer got to his feet and walked over to the Breton, grabbed him by the beard, and jerked his head forward so that they were almost nose to nose, and rasped: "She aint fer sale, she belongs to me. Now if ye know what's good for yer ye'll back off."

Delattre's face darkened with fury as he pulled away from Rimmer, rose to his feet and walked away toward the aft of the boat.

Believing that he had successfully warned Delattre off, Rimmer returned to the group of men and continued his conversation. A short while later Isaiah spotted Delattre striding back down the deck toward Rimmer's back, arm outstretched with a primed flintlock pistol in his left hand.

"Josh! To your left!" barked Isaiah.

The ball fizzed past Rimmer's neck, missing by a hair's breadth, as he lurched to the right before it thudded and splintered into the oak planking of the deck. A blue powder haze drifted across the deck.

Laying on his side and propped by his right arm, in one movement, Rimmer whipped the Collier from his belt and fired. The ball took Delattre in the lower jaw, angling upward and exiting through his cheek.

Spitting shattered teeth and with blood pulsing from his open mouth, Delattre gave a roar, discarded his pistol, and believing Rimmer had to reload, pulled a skinning knife and came on.

Rimmer quickly spun the chamber of the Collier and fired a second shot. This time the ball took Delattre through the heart and stopped him in his tracks. His blade fell and teetering on his heels for a few seconds, he toppled back onto the deck, like a felled oak, stone dead.

A grin slowly spread across Rimmer's features as he gazed with admiration at the blued steel of the smoking Collier in his left hand, and the seasoned stoics around him sucked on their pipes and grunted with approval, and shocked missionaries made the sign of the cross.

"Bury 'im, boy," rasped Rimmer, nodding to Isaiah and gesturing toward the river. And so, summoning all his strength, Isaiah heaved Delattre's huge bloodied hulk of a body over the side.

9

After twenty two days the Floridiana finally reached Fort Leavenworth, where it remained moored for refuelling before embarking on the final stretch of its journey to Fort Pierre on the edge of the Black Hills.

At least another seventeen days' river journey was still ahead of it.

Rimmer stocked up with provisions of army hard tack and biscuits before the Floridiana set off once more.

The beauty of the land and sky continued to inspire Isaiah. He filled the hours by making drawings and writing descriptions in his journal.

Mostly the dawn would break bright to reveal a late spring sky of sparkling clarity, and never was air so pure that could be drunk so deep to fill the lungs with exhilaration.

Cumulus banking skies would give way to sunsets of furnace crimson, flame orange streaked with pearl grey, turquoise and gold.

The remainder of the journey passed relatively calmly without further fights or killings; remarkable considering the toxic mix of semi-wild trappers and hunters who had been tolerating each other's company for weeks.

It was Rimmer's intention to trek overland to the land of the Flat Heads in order to trade for ponies. Most trappers rode mules. Rimmer, however, preferred the more nimble Indian pony.

The final stretch of the river journey was by flat-boat along the Belle Fourche and after this it would be overland to the Bighorn, through the land of the Shoshone to Trout Peak, and finally to Absaroka.

The early June weather remained sultry, however after a number of days a cooler south-easterly wind began to form giant dark banks of cloud which rolled across the plains, bringing rain and deep pounding thunder. Fork lightning sheared and jagged the horizon.

For two days the storm lashed and sheeted the land, turning tracks into quagmires and rivulets.

After a few miles of the land trek Isaiah's old and worn oilskin cape began to let water and his wide-brimmed felt hat became so sodden it began to droop. His undubbed leather boots gradually saturated through to his skin and for the first time a sense of desolation took him. By contrast Rimmer and Watseka appeared comfortable in their buffalo robes, animal skin hoods and thick rawhide, heavily-tallowed moccasins.

The Flathead village was shielded by rocky outcrops and clusters of Grey Elder.

The tracks into the village had been churned into a mass of boot-clawing mud and pony shit.

The rain eventually became finer, turning to a vaporous mist which gusted across the Indian lodges and mingled with woodsmoke from the numerous fires, permeating an atmosphere of grey gloom. They passed two half-starved dogs tearing at a discarded carcass of bones in the mud. An old woman emerged from one of the lodges carrying a bone war club. She walked over to the dogs and proceeded to beat one to death by bludgeoning its skull to a bloody pulp. Shit spurted from its backside as it screamed, yelped and gagged with each blow. She then gathered the dead animal by its hind legs and dragged it back to her lodge.

"Game must be scarce," Rimmer muttered, as they passed rows of dead black crows hanging by their claws from poles, their feathers bedraggled and dripping.

As the three made their way through the centre of the village to the lodge of the headman, the extraordinary form of a deformed holy man seemed to appear from nowhere and crab-shuffle across their path carrying the head of a dead viper. Without moving his head he flashed an askance leer and then vanished into the drifting mist.

Isaiah's low mood began to provoke nostalgic recollections of home; of hot meals, and his sisters in fits of laughter at supper during times of their father's absence, and of winter evenings by a roaring fire with his mother and Clara. Then a sudden reality check jolted him back to the grey mirk of the Flathead village as the old headman Tse beckoned for them to enter his lodge.

Rimmer was well-acquainted with the old man, having traded with the Flatheads many times in the past.

Tse wore a blanket round his shoulders. His silver hair hung lank to his waist and his face appeared to replicate the fissures and crevices of the red sandstone rocky outcrops that rose from the ground to form distant canyons.

A fire crackled in the centre of the lodge. A yellowish-grey broth with surface scum bubbled in a cast iron kettle that was suspended over the fire on an iron bar. The broth smelled of boiling fat and bones and its odour mingled with the woodsmoke to produce a noxious haze. It clawed at Isaiah's nostrils and tainted the back of his throat.

The flames illuminated the hide walls of the lodge with flickering light.

Shadows danced on an array of spirit totems, animal skins and the heads of wolves.

Four other village elders joined the old headman and sat in a circle around the fire. A pipe was passed and then Rimmer, communicating in sign, informed Tse that he had come to trade for ponies. The Flatheads were renowned pony herders and Rimmer valued their judgement of horse flesh.

Watseka then emptied two canvas rolls of trade quality hatchets, hunting knives and quids of chewing tobacco onto the ground.

Tse eyed the pile with an air of disinterest. Rimmer frowned, sat back, sucked on his pipe, thought for a moment, then removed an oiled greaseproof paper wrapping from a small percussion pistol inlaid with brass, with a polished walnut stock.

Tse's expression brightened as he handled the tiny weapon and ran his fingers over its smooth, well-worked surfaces, and then nodded to Rimmer with satisfaction indicating that here was the basis of a good trade.

Shortly after, a stooped elderly woman with long grey-brown hair hanging loose, entered the lodge and began ladling the boiling unsavoury broth into carved wooden bowls and handed one to each person seated round the fire.

Isaiah stared down at the contents of his bowl with revulsion. Scum had settled on the edge of the bowl. Pieces of fat, gristle and what appeared to be some kind of root floated in the watery grey liquid.

"Down it, boy! They'll be offended if ye don't," whispered Rimmer.

Isaiah put the bowl to his lips and took a mouthful, and in a struggle not to retch he swallowed. He gulped down water with each mouthful in an attempt to wash down the rancidity and the lingering aftertaste.

At the end of the meal a pipe was passed once again and Rimmer continued his dialogue in sign. Then after a short while the lodge fell silent as the crippled form of the Shaman entered.

He was extremely revered within Flathead society and considered to have been touched by spirits by dint of his deformities. They called him Wakanda, the possessor of powers.

He was hunched and barely five feet tall. He wore a robe adorned with a thousand feathers. His black, lank, tallowed hair was woven with dried animal parts and hung low. His complexion was dark, almost reptilian, and the jutting beak-like form of his head resembled a bird of prey.

His eyes flickered and darted like the flames of the fire, and all who saw him sensed the force of his extraordinary presence.

He circled the fire and began a chant in a voice

that sounded like rooks cawing at dusk. He tossed an obscure mixture into the flames and they flared higher in intense blue and soft violet. An oil of camphor and burning fat-like vapour began to drift low through the lodge.

It began to induce in Isaiah a sense of unreality as his vision blurred, his thoughts began to scramble, and nausea pulsed in his throat.

The flames of the fire began to writhe and twist as if in agony, and in the atmosphere of the lodge he sensed the portend to forces being summoned.

Wakanda then appeared to scoop embers from the fire with his bare hands, yet no odour of burning flesh emanated, and through the flames Watseka's face began to shimmer then vanish and then appear again.

Then with tiny childlike hands he turned to Isaiah and gestured; and in a croaking voice delivered harsh words to Tse, and with that he leapt over the flames and disappeared into the darkening damp village.

Tse frowned as he translated Wakanda's words to Rimmer.

"Crippled coon reckons a bad spirit treads in yer shadow and death waits, wants us gone by first light," Rimmer muttered, turning to Isaiah.

Mystified, Isaiah dismissed Wakanda's utterances as nothing more than the Shaman's superstitious ramblings. However, as he stared into the flames goose flesh crawled on his neck and the broth began to reflux in his gullet.

That night they slept in an adjacent lodge. Isaiah was restless with his intermittent sleep disturbed by churning dreams. He woke halfway through the night with the unsavoury broth surging dyspeptic in his chest.

He got up and stumbled out into the cool night. The air tingled in his nostrils as he retched onto the ground. He then returned to the lodge, drank deep from his water sack, lay back on his robe and slept deep.

Laying beside Watseka, his senses even in sleep triggered by movement Rimmer observed him one-eyed with a faint smile.

The next thing he knew was Rimmer shaking him from a deep sleep.

"C'mon, boy, we have ter make tracks."

Feeling liverish, with his tongue thick and his mouth dry, Isaiah got to his feet.

It was first light and the village was strangely silent. The rain had ceased and the mist was gradually lifting. Clawing woodsmoke had been replaced by a fresh earthy damp fragrance. The grey eastern sky was streaked with hazy ribs of cream light.

Three sleek-looking ponies had been tethered outside the lodge. Watseka had already mounted and with the pack mule in tow, was skilfully controlling her pony's friskiness.

As they rode back down the rock and scrub-lined muddy track that led out of the village, a faint wailing met their ears. They all turned, and there, to the east, on a distant rise, stood the Shaman, crooked arms raised to the sky, and silhouetted against the yellow dawn.

"Homage ter the four winds," murmured Rimmer as they rode on.

10

As the days went by the Shaman's warning continued to dog Isaiah's thoughts, and Rimmer began to sense it.

"Don't allow them words of that crippled coon ter play on yer mind, boy. It's all hokum. Just believe in what ye can touch, hear'n see, and ye won't go far wrong."

Rimmer's natural pragmatism eventually jolted Isaiah out of his persistent mood, and together with the warmth of the sun, his spirits lifted.

In the land of the Shoshone they camped in hidden ravines, in secluded Aspen copses at the foot of bluffs, and by streams in dense forests of pine.

Rimmer occasionally picked up Indian signs in the form of hunting party tracks, however they encountered no human life. Rimmer always seemed to know how old the tracks were and who had made them.

They shot and roasted a variety of game from Sage Grouse, Snowshoe Hare, and Jackrabbit.

When game was scarce Watseka cooked up a tolerably palatable hash of the hard tack and biscuits Rimmer had acquired at Leavenworth.

Small game, however, could not satisfy Rimmer's craving for big meat, and on one late afternoon he spotted a set of tracks running east.

The low sun cast shadows on heart-shaped hoof prints in the dry dust. He inspected small piles of dark brown plum-like turds.

"Deer run, White-tails, small herd, aint long passed! We'll eat good tonight."

They followed the tracks for around an hour along a rock-strewn, dusty trail until they reached a spruce-lined meadow and there they were, in the distance, their reddish brown coats in shadow under low branches, grazing on early summer meadow grass.

They dismounted.

Watseka remained well back with the mounts. With primed Hawkens, Rimmer and Isaiah approached in stealth. They reached a low rocky ridge and crouched down. The evening was sultry with no hint of a breeze. The deer sensed nothing.

"Take a bead on the doe on the far left," whispered Rimmer.

The click of the Hawken hammer startled the deer and their heads jerked upward, and the whites of their undertails flashed in the shadows.

Then suddenly, as Isaiah squeezed the trigger and the rifle recoiled into his shoulder, they turned and bolted, the young doe with them.

"Shit!" Rimmer barked.

Then the doe faltered. She staggered, her legs crumpled and she slowly sank, belly down.

"By fuck you got 'er, boy!"

Isaiah reached the doe first. The kill had not been a clean one. Shot through the lower abdomen, she lay in agony, struggling to right herself, her eyes glazed liquid with fear.

Isaiah gazed at her, transfixed with pity, until Rimmer jerked the doe's head back and quickly ran the blade of his Green River across her throat. Blood gushed onto the long grass and then she slumped lifeless.

"Aint no room for sentiment, boy. We have ter eat!"

That night they camped under a low escarpment in the lea of a freshening wind.

Watseka skinned and quartered the doe, then roasted the choicest cuts. She fried the liver and kidneys with wild garlic, which she foraged nearby, in belly fat, and boiled a quart of coffee.

They ate royally that evening.

Flavoured with woodsmoke and bubbling bark resins, they gorged on the fat-dribbling meat.

After they had eaten, for once Rimmer said little. Well-satisfied he basked in the glow of the fire, smoked his pipe and drank his coffee.

The following morning they rode the base of the escarpment for miles until they reached more densely wooded country of Juniper and Grey Elder. A wide stream ran north-west skirting the edges of woodland. They watered their ponies and refilled their water sacks.

Honed in the wild, Rimmer's senses were feral, and his powers of anticipation uncanny. Odours and subtle vibrations in wind change would occasionally flare his nostrils and his responses would sometimes equate to warnings, and not long after they had remounted he gestured for them to back into the cover of trees.

They sat and waited. After a short while a distant pounding met their ears. As it grew louder it was accompanied by the faint jangle of swaying weapons and accoutrements.

White, yellow, tawny grey, and the occasional flash of steel flickered through gaps in the dense foliage on the opposite bank of the stream.

"Hunting party," wheezed Rimmer under his breath.

As they rode on the forest terrain gradually became more dense, and by late afternoon the ponies became skittish and began to toss their heads nervously.

Rimmer sensed something some distance away, his nostrils widening in a grimace.

The forest glade was putrid with death; two men lay mouldering in their own dried blood. Carrion crows pecking at their carcasses flew off as the ponies broke through the trees.

There was a stark contrast in the manner the two men had met their deaths. One had been stripped naked and tied to stakes in the ground with rawhide. Blowflies crawled over the bloody scalped mass that had once formed the top of his head. His eyes had been cut from their sockets and hung from tiny nerve threads. His arms had been slashed from shoulder to wrist and his thighs laid open to the knee. A fine shaft had been rammed down his urethra so that his penis appeared to stand erect, and his entire body was streaked with rivulets of congealed blood. The forest grass beneath him was saturated with the dark stain of body fluid and haemorrhage.

The other man lay propped against a tree fully clothed. An arrow had been shot at point blank range into his chest piercing his heart. It had been shot with such force that a third of the shaft protruded beneath his left shoulder blade.

He had died with his eyes open and blood that

had surged from his chest through his nostrils had matted in his grey beard.

Rimmer dismounted and knelt beside the man.

"Knowed him from Rendezvous. English Aug they called him. Bah all accounts he murdered 'is wife and fled ter the mountains ter escape English law. Coons didn't cut 'im outta respect for 'is bravery. T'other one must have pleaded for 'is life and cried for 'is mother."

He studied the ground beyond the glade and discovered mule dung and the tracks of around ten ponies running south-west. Watseka inspected the flight feathers of the arrow embedded in the Englishman's chest.

"Pawnee!" Her voice barely a sigh in the low breeze.

Rimmer grunted. "Same coons as passed us awhile back. Must have crossed the stream at some point, kilt these men and stole thar pack mules, more'an likely plew-laden."

They rode on.

They reached Absaroka in early October. They had ridden through valleys and meadows lush from dew and late summer rains. After chill nights under robes they woke to crisp sparkling dawns in forested mountain passes touched here and there with russet and blood red.

And not for the first time was Isaiah stirred to contemplate the notion of paradise, both in relation to wondrous consciousness, and the concept manipulated as a kind of bribe for an eternal afterlife entitled only to those judged as righteous. There were times when he would lay awake under his robe, restless with ideas; the silence of the night broken only by the occasional distant scream of prey being taken, or the wind roaring through rocky gullies and dense woodland.

Whenever possible they camped by streams, and one morning just after dawn, while Rimmer sipped his coffee and drew on his first pipe of the day, Watseka slipped away through the trees upstream. Some minutes later, feeling the stirring of his bowels, Isaiah made his way into the trees in the same direction.

Some distance from the camp he spotted Watseka through a gap in the foliage, squatting in the water of the stream, her skirt gathered to her waist, cleansing herself; the clear mountain water clouding from her menstruation.

The early morning light glinted on her hair and highlighted the curves of her buttocks, and at that moment he thought her nothing less than integral to the very land that procured her, and the very essence of primal womanhood.

Thoughts of taking her there and then in that wilderness caused his manhood to stiffen.

Transfixed, he watched her climb out of the stream, sit on the bank and dry her powerful legs, her pubic hair and groin. He watched her form a pad and secure it between her legs with a soft doeskin harness which she tied round her waist.

She then threw her blanket over her shoulders and made her way back to the camp and Rimmer.

Then struggling to suppress his guilt-laden desires, Isaiah made his way deeper into the trees in the opposite direction. Shame racked him as he relieved himself; shame at his voyeurism in spying on a private moment, and shame that he had committed a kind of moral betrayal to his mentor.

When Isaiah arrived back, Rimmer and Watseka were preparing to break camp, and to his relief Rimmer appeared in buoyant mood. Isaiah flushed as he threw a glance at Watseka, as they mounted their ponies. She returned his glance with a faint smile that was nothing less than telling. Then they all rode on.

Days from the end of their journey they emerged from the final mountain pass into a serene valley of waist-high grasses that swayed, undulated and whispered in the wind which gusted now from the northwest, bringing with it billowing cloud and oppressive skies.

At the end of the valley, rising granite cliffs ran for miles in each direction like a great fortress monolith appearing to bar the way of travellers.

After they had crossed the valley Rimmer led them towards what appeared from a distance to be a dark gash in the granite face. As they approached it became clear that the dark slash was a narrow passageway through the immense face of the cliff wall.

"They call this the Kamali Canyon of the spirit guide. Legend tells that a force dwells here that guides the spirits of warriors who died bravely to the afterlife. The place is sacred, to the Crow, they seldom come here. It's a shortcut; saves more'an a hundred miles."

Rimmer's voice sounded hollow as they entered the mouth of the canyon.

An oppressive tension pulsed across Isaiah's temples, and strange fluttering sensations brushed his forehead.

"Something's here, Josh, I feel it!" murmured Isaiah as he spurred his pony.

"Keep ridin', boy. No harm'll come to ye."

Also not for the first time had Watseka ridden the Kamali and sensed its presence.

She remained hunched in the saddle, her robe pulled tightly around her, her head bowed, not looking left or right.

The air was still in spite of a strong wind gusting out on the flat lands. There was also a permeating odour of dry dust and stagnant pools, combined with a lingering, choking void that sometimes portends death.

The silence of the Kamali was broken only by the echo of the ponies' hooves grinding on dry shale and granite dust.

The passageway through was barely forty feet at its widest and approximately twelve feet at its narrowest. It twisted and turned through the great dark granite walls which rose hundreds of feet to the bright slit of sky above. Buzzards soared high in the teeth of the north-westerly as if waiting for those who dared ride the Kamali to perish. Two broken skulls, pecked clean, stared down from a ledge around thirty feet from the ground.

Halfway through claustrophobic sensations began to grip Isaiah causing his palms to sweat. He rode ahead endeavouring to conceal his nervousness, lest Rimmer should become aware, and then glancing up to the distant canyon rim he caught sight of tiny moving figures silhouetted against the light. However, the vision was fleeting and when he looked again they were gone.

After a two mile ride through the Kamali's tortuous path, the three emerged with some relief into a lush, fertile basin shielded on all sides by bluffs from fierce winds. A distant waterfall fed a tree-lined, winding stream that ran west; a paradise contrastingly juxtaposed to the dark, foreboding passageway.

Rimmer turned to Isaiah as they rode: "Like I said, saves around a hundred mile; heard some Crow talk of that canyon as an almighty wound that never heals. Interestin', eh boy!"

And with that they crossed the basin in early evening light, heading toward the final mountain pass that led to the track to Rimmer's cabin.

Strange structures silhouetted against the skyline on the eastern bluff caught Isaiah's eye as they rode closer. Horizontal forms lay on log platforms. Bird-like shapes and feathers writhed and fluttered in the wind.

"Crow burial ground," growled Rimmer. "Sacred ground. We'll need to give that a wide berth outta respect. Violate thar burial ground and they'll hunt ye down."

It was dusk when they finally ascended the mountain track that led to Rimmer's cabin.

Sometime after Rimmer had quit the Hudson's Bay Company and became a free trapper, he threw in his lot with a mountain man called Jacob Smead, and it was during his partnership with Smead that both men built the mountain log cabin.

Smead was an experienced, skilled trapper. At that time he was a man in middle-age, and had spent all of his adult life in the mountains, and knew little of civilisation. He was uneducated and illiterate. He was, however, a fierce, cruel fighter and had developed a reputation as an obsessional Indian hater. He had been known to behead his victims in roaring bloodlust after scalping them; a practice even Rimmer found distasteful.

Rimmer's partnership with Smead, however, was short-lived; it lasted just over a year. Smead's reputation finally caught up with him. He and Rimmer were ambushed one winter's evening by a party of Bloods, a number of whom in the past Smead had taken great pleasure in butchering.

Smead was fifty-four years old when he was run through with lances from two sides simultaneously by two warriors. After wounding one warrior with a shot from his Hawken, Rimmer took off and managed to escape with his life.

The Bloods, however, captured Rimmer and Smead's mules, both laden with high quality plews and skins.

After Smead's demise Rimmer joined forces with a Dutch trapper called Van Bork. He was younger than Smead and a fine mountain man. Quiet and thoughtful, he was a complete contrast to the brutal Smead and he and Rimmer forged an admirable relationship.

Again, the union did not last. After only six months Van Bork was gored in the thigh during a hunt by a charging buffalo cow endeavouring to protect her calf. He did manage to shoot the cow, and he and Rimmer ate well that evening. However, within two weeks, Van Bork was dead from septicaemia.

After the death of his second partner Rimmer decided to go it alone, and in due course, as a result of his liaison and trading with the Crow, he met and married the Crow beauty Watseka.

Rimmer and Smead had chosen well with regard to the siting of their cabin; accessed by a mountain track around a quarter of a mile long, it nestled against a southern precipice on a tree-ridged plateau overlooking a wooded valley of Aspen, pine, and Blue Spruce. In the lea of the northern passes it was sheltered from the killer northers of deep winter.

Two hundred yards to the west of the cabin was a tiny waterfall that cascaded gently down onto a deep ledge of rock pools, providing the cabin with constant fresh mountain water. Built from caulked spruce and pine logs, Rimmer and Smead had achieved a rugged, sturdy, weatherproof construction.

The cabin consisted of two bunk rooms, a large living space, with a huge drystone fireplace in which cast iron pots were suspended on a spit-iron. The floor was compacted dirt, and gun racks, hunting trophies, furs, skins and Indian scalps adorned the walls. To the side of the cabin was a small coral and an outhouse in which Rimmer stored his traps, pelts and various tools.

By mountain standards the snows were not severe that winter, hence killing time between November and late March, when the trapping season began, was made more tolerable, and numerous hunting trips relieved periods of boredom.

Before the "Willow Killer", the first real cold of the winter, they journeyed to the winter village of the Crow so that Watseka could consult the Shaman and seek his power to banish the spirit hawk that dogged her dreams.

The hawk repeatedly returned. Her dream sequence was always the same. From a searing light it would emerge; at first a tiny speck, and then in flight it grew larger and larger, finally to envelope in suffocating blackness, and its meaning remained an enigma.

That year the Crow winter camp was at the foot of Trout Peak on the Shoshone, a ride of about eighty miles.

They set off at dawn, riding into an easterly breeze which brought with it intermittent flurries of snow. They arrived at the Crow village at the hour before dusk; a fine dusting of snow now covered the land. The village was large, around eighty to ninety tipis scattered along the Shoshone River. Heavily armed, dark, high-cheek-boned outriders with loose hanging hair, dressed in furs and skins escorted them in. Rimmer was well-known to the Crow and there was a great deal of laughter and banter as they rode.

Watseka's mood appeared to lift at the prospect of reunion with her own people, and she displayed a surprising contrast to her usual quiet, withdrawn demeanour as she shrieked with laughter at some of the off-the-cuff remarks from the Crow riders.

The Crow village was little different to the dismal Flathead camp with its general strewn detritus and half-starved dogs fighting over mouldering bones on the freezing horseshit-scattered ground.

The cold evening air was charged with woodsmoke and the fumes of burning flesh. Gangs of darting raven-haired children followed the ponies to the centre of the village. One of them threw a tiny wooden lance which narrowly missed Isaiah's shoulder. The boy then ran off shrieking with laughter.

Tipi fires glimmered in the fading light, and here and there amongst the tipis black meat hung on drying racks amid dismembered carcasses piled high on beds of bloodied branches.

The village bustled with activity; numerous women were going about their early evening business. An intermittent stream of riders came in from hunting trips. One was distinctive and caught the eye as he rode by. His shoulder-length hair was light brown and his skin was not deeply toned. Yet he possessed the high, broad cheek bones and the long Roman nose of the Crow. He was clean-shaven, save for a small tuft of beard under his lower lip. A clutch of river trout hung from the pommel of his saddle. He nodded an acknowledgement to Rimmer and Isaiah as he cantered by.

"Breed," Rimmer muttered. "White blood thar, no question. Aint never seen him afore."

As a race the Crows were handsome and Isaiah was moved to admire them.

"Aint no red coons finer," quipped Rimmer. "Thar bead 'n hide work's second to none."

They rode to the tipi of Ujarek, Watseka's father. Her younger sister Tamaya beckoned them in.

Ujarek sat on robes in front of a central fire. He did not get to his feet when Rimmer entered, he merely grunted in recognition when Rimmer squatted next to him and placed his hand across his chest. Ujarek had been handsome in his youth, however recent years of addiction to trade liquor had taken their toll and he looked older than his fifty-five years. His body was bloated, and his eyes were shot with blood and were running to jaundice.

Tamaya's similarity to Watseka was striking, although less than her equal in looks. Slightly shorter in stature, her black hair was parted in the centre and hung in tightly plaited braids with the ends bound with beaded thongs. She wore a neck piece decorated with elk teeth. Numerous rings adorned her fingers and her heavily-fringed deerskin robe trailed the ground.

That evening Watseka learned of her mother's death, killed during a buffalo hunt the previous spring. On the journey to Rimmer's cabin, when in sight of the Crow burial ground, she had unwittingly ridden past her mother's hide-swaddled body, facing skyward toward her journey to an eternal afterlife.

There she lay on her burial platform, her possessions fluttering in the wind like groping gestures, reaching.

A central fire roared and crackled in Ujarek's great hide lodge; the woodsmoke rising into the night through the high smoke flaps.

Before alcohol had dulled his senses Ujarek had been a great hunter. Wolf's heads, elk horns and the skull of a cougar hung from the lodge poles.

Night had fallen by the time they sat in a circle on robes round the fire. More of Watseka's relatives entered the lodge. Two young men, both in their prime, full of bravado, sat opposite Isaiah and Rimmer.

A village elder, an old man with shoulder-length hair the colour of dull, yellowed steel, with fingers missing on his left hand, sat next to Ujarek.

He lost his fingers during a raid on the Crow village by Blackfeet many years earlier; a black day in Crow history with many young men lost, lodges burned, women dragged off as slaves, children's skulls smashed with war clubs and babies spiked on lances. And those who survived the raid found it harrowing to recall.

Rimmer presented two hand-carved ivory and maple pipes in a wooden case to Ujarek; a gift which provoked little reaction from the stony-faced old man.

As was his way, Rimmer talked incessantly in Crow, with his ramblings at times sparking much laughter.

Two women then entered carrying a large steaming kettle and hung it on an iron crossbar which bridged the embers, filling the lodge with the fatty odour of boiled, stuffed buffalo entrails.

By contrast to the swill served up by the Flatheads, Isaiah found the Crow meal delicately flavoursome.

After the meal conversation continued late into the night with more visitors joining the gathering as news of Rimmer's arrival spread through the village.

The following morning Watseka and the village Shaman rode out at dawn. Hoar frost had gripped the land and the air bit raw with cold.

The Shaman was old; his true age was unknown. Time had little meaning amongst the Crow, yet for an ancient his lean body was not stooped.

Almost blind, his eyes were clouded by milky

veils. His tawny cheeks were hollow and his lipless mouth merely a fine line.

He wore a wolf's head cap and a huge buffalo robe with the fur turned inward. The ringed beak of an eagle hung from a thong round his neck. He carried a sacred looped crook that had been handed down through generations and was believed to be imbued with energy. He was revered for his wisdom, his insight and the enigmatic reach of his senses. In his time he had healed wounds with biorhythmic chanting, herbal potions that drew out sepsis, and the power of will.

They rode to a high plateau that was considered sacred, not far from the burial ground. Watseka then knelt on the frozen ground. The Shaman lit a fire with dry tinder and with his crook he dragged a circle round the fire and the kneeling Watseka. He then began a warbling, moaning chant and with his arms made gestures which drew out smoke forms from the embers.

He then placed Watseka's wingless hawk into the flames where it appeared to writhe, twist and spit before it was engulfed in a vortex of smoke.

After an hour of chanting Watseka's head jerked upward, and with her mouth gaping she moaned as the Shaman drew out a corner of her subconscious.

Then to the east the cream-grey blanket of sky was suddenly punctured with a hole of pale light which slowly, insidiously crept over and washed the land.

As the flames of the fire died the Shaman broke the sacred circle and Watseka rose up. Within the smouldering ash lay the distorted, peeling, grey-black form of the wingless hawk. As the eastern light edged slowly over the land the dense cloud began to disperse, and with it came a strong easterly breeze.

Flurries of sleet now stung Watseka's cheeks as she faced the bitter wind and her thick black-grey hair danced wild as the wind took it.

The Shaman then struck the charred hawk and destroyed its shape and form and as he did so the increasing wind lifted its ash like an ethereal cloud over Watseka and then high toward the western sky, flecking her hair and her body.

The old Shaman then finally instructed her to return to the village and the lodge of her father.

After she had ridden away he remained in the sacred circle for hours, baring his spare and withered torso to the cutting wind, arms raised to give thanks and pay homage to the forces summoned.

Exhausted and drawn from the exorcism, Watseka slept for the remainder of that day in Ujarek's lodge, and then on through the night.

Perhaps from now on in the delirium of her dreams the spirit hawk would be banished forever.

. . .

After some weeks spent in the Crow camp, the arrival of the Cold Moon saw Rimmer, Watseka and Isaiah make their way back through deepening snows to Rimmer's cabin to "winter out" and prepare for spring trapping.

11

> I do not remember where we camped that winter but it must have been a time of peace and plenty to eat.
> – Black Elk, Holy Man.

Numerous hunting trips punctuated the long winter months. They trekked almost daily in Crow-style snow shoes down into the lower valleys to inspect the traps and snares Rimmer had laid. The bounty of small game the traps yielded fluctuated. Some days nothing, others a fox, a snowshoe hare, a racoon or a red squirrel.

They would trek through meadows, forests and

passes, through gentle flurries and blizzard squalls where vision blurred in the ice-laden wind and then on through majestic cloud breaks when sunlight moved its gentle surge to reveal the crisp, sparkling brilliance of the white land.

The chestnut-brown hide of the ageing cow punched a black hole in the blinding white of the meadow. Somehow separated from her herd she foraged in the snow-laden branches of the edge of deep-lined spruce. Bellowing occasionally as she moved, her hot breath vaporised in the cold air.

They were four hundred yards from her and she was oblivious to their presence.

"Upwind."

Rimmer nodded and they moved in an arc into the soft breeze, encircling her.

"She's weak."

Going down on one knee, crouching and taking aim, the report of the Hawken reverberated through the blanket silence of the valley.

The cow shuddered and remained frozen and still. Then after seconds her legs crumpled and she slumped, rolling sideways onto the powdered ground, her crimson steaming blood gushing an expanding wound in the snow. Her eyes were wild and her nostrils glistened with mucous.

"She may be tough eatin', she aint young," Rimmer muttered as they approached her.

With his long-bladed Green River, Rimmer cut

across the cow's belly, then over her tail and round her neck, peeling and slicing the hide back to reveal steaming muscle and sinew as he worked, finally releasing the whole hide as one sheet. They then laid it bloody, steaming and flecked with fat onto the frozen ground.

Rimmer cut as many steaks as he could carry, carefully butchering with the grain of the muscle so that the meat would not fall apart when Watseka sliced it into strips.

He finally cut into the great vein-laced, white-blue mound of the cow's stomach. Steaming bile and blood gushed onto the snow dissolving it to the grass, and then removing the liver he sliced it hot into strips, poured over the mustard-like liquid from the gall bladder and ate. Isaiah tentatively chewed on the acid-tainted pungent raw liver, grimaced, heaved and then spat it onto the snow, and Rimmer quietly smirked.

Then heavily-laden with fresh meat they made their way back to the cabin, the weeping, dripping hide lashed to Isaiah's back, and there Watseka fleshed, scraped and prepared it.

During the long winter wait she roasted or boiled all the game that Rimmer and Isaiah slaughtered; even fox, which she boiled in its own blood with water, dried thyme and sage until its fat rimmed the surface of the iron kettle and the meat fell from the bone.

Evening talk was mostly of beaver and trappers' tales, and with such wealth in time Isaiah was able to spend long hours at his journal.

There were times when the tedium of the winter wait began to irritate Rimmer. He would become moody and critical, occasionally picking on Watseka and blaming her for such things as stringy meat or dry tobacco; and once on a hunting trip he fiercely berated Isaiah for missing a sitting deer with a wayward rifle shot.

"Should a knowed better'n throw in ma lot with a green youth," he muttered.

One virtue, however, of Rimmer's character was that his moods were always short-lived and for years Watseka had bore them like the true stoic that she was.

Each night images of Watseka lying naked under a robe with Rimmer would churn restless in Isaiah's thoughts. Through many nights testosterone surges in his young body would deny him sleep. And although the chill of the cabin caused vapourous breath, he would occasionally wake saturated with sweat and long for the dawn.

Then charged with the hot blood of youth he would split logs at first light, naked to the waist, his chest steaming in the raw morning; each powerful stroke of the axe expelling frustration born of seemingly futile desire.

Then energy spent, he would walk through the

trees to the precipice edge and gaze at the rim of the world where the soft glow of eastern light would illuminate the white caps and the rolling purple-green blanket of spruce and elder in the mist-laden passes. Sublime was the land, yet longing racked him still.

After the passing of the winter months, at the beginning of the Pink Moon, there were signs; signs in the changing light, signs when the east wind began to lose its strength, signs when the snows began their insidious recession, signs when the air seemed to tremor with a subtle nuance of renewal, signs when the valleys and the lower peaks were touched with shimmer, signs of a euphoric awakening that coursed through and touched all living things. Isaiah sensed it and felt its energy.

The passing months had also seen a gradual transformation in Isaiah's appearance. He now towered six feet three in his bare feet. His blonde hair touched his shoulders and his heavy beard laced his chest. He wore an antelope skin shirt, leather breeches with smoked buffalo skin leggings, and thick hide moccasins with the fur turned inwards and when out hunting, a buffalo robe coat and an otter skin cap. For Isaiah the skilled hand of Watseka had been so productive.

Rimmer had his informers; Crow hunters whom he had always plied with gifts who knew of obscure streams and tributaries in the north-west that had not been trapped out and were still rich in beaver and otter. However, the hunters urged caution; they were located near the land of the Blackfeet.

And so it was that at first light, days after the dawn of the Pink Moon, Rimmer and Isaiah set off towards the north-west.

They would be gone for months and would therefore leave Watseka with her relatives at the Crow village. She would rejoin them in the Buck Moon when they would make their way to Rendezvous at Green River, near Horse Creek, Wyoming.

They rode with two pack mules. Their accoutrements consisted of beaver traps, a wooden bait box, bullet pouches, fire-making implements, blankets, and spare pairs of moccasins. Sheathed butcher knives, and hatchets were fastened to the pommels of their saddles. Also hanging from Rimmer's saddle was a tobacco sack and a pouch containing numerous pipes.

12

It was late in the Flower Moon and the gentle current of the stream formed eddies round their tallowed calves as they laid the traplines that would be their last that spring.

Isaiah had worked tirelessly and stoically, never deviating from Rimmer's instructions. The spring squalls interspersed by bursts of searing sun, and the late life that briefly returned to winter's dying breath in the form of fleeting snows could not temper the force of his energy and the power of his endurance in the perpetual icy streams.

For weeks Watseka's presence had bewitched him to a pitch of irrational obsession. Now her absence had left a strange void of relief that dwelt in the irony of longing and compulsion that fuelled his strength.

Indeed, so primed was he that Rimmer began to

wonder what drove him. Not that Rimmer was in any way concerned. The preceding weeks had been a time of bounty that had exceeded his expectations.

They had walked and rode many miles, setting traps and gathering in pelts, amassing two packs of high quality plews, an equal number of inferior pelts, plus around sixty otter skins.

In the evenings they would boil coffee, roast beaver tails and recount the events of the day. Rimmer smoked, rambled incessantly; Isaiah listened and listened while he dubbed the pelts with a piece of sharpened elkhorn, and Rimmer quietly concluded that a man of fewer words than Isaiah he had never before encountered.

The stream was deep, wide and gently flowing. Heavy undergrowth and trees grew profusely in an arch on both banks, meeting above to form a dense tunnel-like canopy that stretched downstream to where it curved and the foliage became more sparse and a hole of sunlight burned like a torch. There was a track the width of two ponies that ran down one of its banks.

The water of the stream was clear. Minnows glistened silver as they darted and zig-zagged against the current. Eels and catfish lurked in the dark silt and moss-covered overhangs of fallen trees and projecting rocks. Further upstream it forked, became wider, and the banks became more rocky and the foliage less dense, and here were the enmeshed branches and the dam of twigs, and here the beaver teemed.

All appeared calm; the breeze gently caressed the leaves, the water occasionally slapped the steep banks, a bird screeched as it flew up into higher branches.

They were downwind of the current and Rimmer stiffened; he rose up from his work, his jaw clenched and his head jerked suddenly in the direction of downstream, nostrils widening. He then gestured to Isaiah with a degree of alarm toward their weapons, the pack mules and the opposite bank.

Responding to Rimmer's gesticulations, he led the animals across the stream and then into deep cover some distance back and tethered them. They then crept forward with Hawkens primed and loaded and waited, well-hidden, spying upstream through gaps in the foliage.

They came from the light from round the bend in the stream; painted, primeval demons, their black cheekbones high below all-seeing savage, slanting eyes. Dark killers armed with bows, hatchets and lances, wretched in their diabolic intent. Five warriors in all, their ponies in peak condition from spring grazing, prancing in the dappled light. Flashes of ochre and vermilion smeared the jangling, glittering vision of them. Bear-greased raven hair bound in topknots, porcupine quill breastplates, hard-hide shields adorned with sacred symbols, on they came, single file along the narrow bank, on they came, blood-chilling.

The lead warrior appeared older than those who followed him. His huge topknot was streaked with grey and bound with otter fur. A slender braided lock hung from his forehead over the left side of his face, and the bear-greased vermilion on his cheek flashed a contrast against the green of the foliage. The right side of his head had been shaved and the ripple of an old battle scar ran from his temple to the base of his jaw. His nose ran sharp, hawk-like down to the thin, mean line of his lips and his nostrils flared intermittently to the impulses of his senses.

He carried a steel-tipped lance adorned with swaying scalp trophies, all blue-black as the night except one, which was thick, long and fair; and from his belt hung a stone war club with a bound hide handle ingrained dark with grease and old blood.

He rasped orders to those who followed him and they grunted and murmured in response.

"Blackfeet," whispered Rimmer.

Isaiah's palms became clammy as he tightened his grip on the stock of his Hawken.

Glancing down into the stream the lead warrior suddenly raised an arm in a signal to halt and gestured down into the water.

"Fuck! Coon's seen the trap. Keep low, boy, till ah give the word," muttered Rimmer under his breath.

The lead warrior then ordered the two braves

behind him to cross the stream. Little more than thirty feet away from Rimmer and Isaiah, they dismounted and made their way through the trees and undergrowth in the direction of the pelt-laden mules.

Discovering the pack mules they then led them back to the stream's bank, their voices staccato in the echoing void of the canopy.

Rimmer waited for them to pass and then gave the nod. Both men then reared and charged. Taken by surprise the warriors attempted to turn and simultaneously grab their weapons. All too late, Rimmer and Isaiah were on them.

Rimmer took the nearest, plunging his knife repeatedly into the warrior's kidneys. The warrior jerked back with a guttural moan and slumped forward. Rimmer then followed up with a neck slash severing deep arteries. Blood jetted in intermittent bursts onto the warrior's chest; he was young, too young.

Isaiah managed to headlock the other warrior. He was lean and strong but no match for Isaiah as he crushed his windpipe with his forearm. Blood bloated his cheeks, his veins pulsed and his eyes bulged wide as the life was choked from him.

This was Isaiah's first kill; a deadly sickening struggle of close combat. He smelled the warrior's rank breath; smelled the bear grease in his lank hair and the tallow in his war paint. He heard the rattle in the warrior's throat as he applied lethal pressure. Then there was the resistant, jerking muscular struggle and the submissive weakening as death took hold.

For a moment nauseous guilt gripped Isaiah; within minutes he had taken a life. Then there was torment; thoughts of the village the warrior would never return to, the hysterical grieving of a mother or wife as Isaiah released the vice-like pressure exerted by his forearm.

Then the torment was wiped as Rimmer ensured death by plunging his knife into the warrior's chest.

Within minutes the lead and fourth warriors reappeared, galloping back on the far bank. They crossed the stream screeching war cries. Shafts of light through the trees played tricks with vision as they came on, dazzling and shimmering as they rode. Rimmer fired his Hawken in a reflex movement. The ball fizzed past the lead warrior's shoulder and crackled through the higher branches. The warrior vaulted from his pony and hurled his lance.

Rimmer shimmied as the lance tore through his shirt and ploughed through the soft flesh above his hip.

Believing that Rimmer's firepower was spent the lead warrior came on now with war club in hand. Like lightning Rimmer pulled the Collier and fired removing the warrior's lower jaw in a spray of blood, shattered teeth and bone. However on he came, now like a screaming, blood-spraying banshee from the nether world. Rimmer fired a second shot, this time at closer range. The ball smashed into the warrior's chest, ripping through the right lung and exiting below the shoulder. The warrior crumpled, rasped a final defiant war cry, and with surging blood flicking the air he toppled back like a felled tree into the stream.

Isaiah ducked behind the pack mules as an arrow thudded into the pelts. Firing his Hawken over the mule's neck, he hit the fourth warrior in the abdomen knocking him off his pony into the stream. Blood clouded the clear water as the warrior crawled to the opposite bank, leaned against a tree and began groaning his death song.

The fifth warrior finally appeared breaking through the trees on the far bank, doubling back after scouting further upstream. The sight of his leader and comrades cut and shot to pieces caused him to lose stomach for a fight, and with a scream of defiance and holding his war club aloft he galloped back downstream towards the light.

Rimmer fired twice in quick succession at the fleeing warrior, however he proved a difficult target, swerving and weaving as he rode and both shots hissed wide.

"Shit!" Rimmer cursed as the warrior disappeared round the bend in the stream from whence he had come.

Rimmer then dropped to his knees as his wound bled more profusely.

"Shut that moanin' fucker up, boy," tossing the Collier to Isaiah. There was one remaining ball in its chamber.

Kill in cold blood! Isaiah recoiled. However, Rimmer's presence seemed to drive him and gripped by a momentary compulsion, and with pulse racing, he took hold of the butt of the Collier and crossed the stream.

The warrior sat propped against a tree. The ground beneath him, his breechclout and thighs were saturated with blood and bile from his seeping gut wound. He was becoming weaker by the minute through loss of blood and his death song began to falter as Isaiah approached. The warrior appeared calm and did not look up. His gaze was fixed on a point in the rippling water, his eyes were wide and unblinking. Isaiah pressed the barrel of the Collier against the warrior's temple and fired. The ball blew the right side of the skull away exposing brain and liquid soft tissue. The warrior slumped forward and Isaiah turned and heaved into the undergrowth.

Rimmer spat with distain and clutching his bleeding side proceeded to take his trophies, ripping the hair from the skulls of the dead braves with repulsive suction and then holding them aloft in triumphant bloodlust.

He doused his wound with whisky and then crudely sewed the two gaping flaps of flesh together with catgut and bound it tight with calico. However, despite the bindings, the wound continued to weep.

With Rimmer's wound causing him some concern, they broke camp late that afternoon, and with pelt-laden pack mules in tow, left the scene of the fight and followed the stream south-west. The journey back to the Crow village would take three days. After around a half a mile the stream widened. A gentle fall gushed down a low precipice into its source. River trout lurked in the shallows and they feasted well on the oily meat.

South-westerly winds brought almost balmy nights and clear dawns of dazzling light.

They rode on through forest glades of ponderosa which eventually became more sparse, giving way to rocky outcrops. They top-rode sandstone ravines with fissures and cracks that resembled the heads and skin of the ancients that had rode before them. Writhing red rock forms appeared to grope upward into eternal space.

In turn the rocky terrain gave way then to rolling valleys and spring meadows glittering with columbine, bergamot and Mountain Aster.

At higher levels they traversed forests of Engelmann Spruce through cooler air. The carcass of a dead moose appeared to bar their way; its flesh stripped spare by wolves and wild dogs, and its ribcage pecked clean by carrion scavengers, shining yellow-grey in the morning light, and the obtuse angle of its great antlers seeming to appear as a chance waymarker directing them on, back south to Absaroka.

It was early evening when they rode into the Crow village. Watseka emerged from her father's lodge to greet them.

With the setting sun at her back, almost ethereal in the smoke-veiled twilight, she stood tall, her hair thick and unplaited, her teeth flashing white in the soft, dark oval of her face as she smiled at Rimmer, and sight of her recharged Isaiah's futile yearning for her and the low apprehension of unfulfillment swamped his emotions once again.

The following day, concern over Rimmer's wound which still seeped led him to visit the Shaman.

The holy man removed Rimmer's coagulated and stained bindings, slowly peeling the calico welded with congealed blood and fluid from Rimmer's side. A ridge of pus oozed from the wound and its lips were florid with oedema.

The Shaman lit a mixture of dried herbs and waved fine fragrant wisps of smoke over the wound and at the same time uttered a low, grating chant.

Rimmer winced as the Shaman cleansed the

wound deep with water and soft doeskin, and applied a poultice of yarrow and bound it with rawhide.

After a number of days at the Crow village they rode out, and then on to Rimmer's cabin. It was time now for reflection, time for recuperation and a time to heal.

It was the first week of the Buck Moon when they rode the high ground out of Absaroka and headed north to Wyoming and Green River.

They rode mountain tracks down to the passes and then on to wide open prairie of larkspur-flecked high grasses that swayed and whispered in a gentle south-westerly.

The prairie stretched for miles to a heat-shimmering purple horizon beneath a great cloudless cerulean sky. In the distance dark smudges of grazing bison punctuated the vast plain, and after an hour's ride they came within range. Rimmer singled out and shot a young bull which Watseka skinned and quartered with startling dexterity and speed; and dripping hump steaks sizzled over their campfire that night.

After a five day ride, it was early evening when they looked down from high ground to the valley of Green River.

Clusters of stained, tawny-coloured tipis lined

the banks of the river. The humid July air was hazy from campfire smoke. Horses, ponies and mules were hobbled amid the trees or grazed in adjoining meadows. The occasional gunshot interrupted a jumbled murmur of harsh voices and faint music.

They rode down a steep track to the river, tethered their ponies and pack mules, and made camp in a clearing away from the main gathering.

Watseka collected kindling, made fire and boiled coffee.

They squatted round the fire, drank coffee and chewed on pemmican.

A group of drunken trappers danced, stomped and roared to a squeezebox tune. Mountain men sat smoking clay and cob pipes round numerous fires, traders haggled, and fat splattered into flames from roasting meat tended by dark, stony-faced Indian women. Rendezvous was in full swing.

"Good ter see ye, Josh. See ye got yeself a big young'un."

"Jacob," Rimmer grunted whilst sipping his coffee and drawing on his pipe.

The lean, animal-skin-clad figure standing behind Watseka was Jacob Troom. Troom was old; to reach three score years and ten when most mountain men did not reach four decades was remarkable.

Constructed of sinew and hard bone, most regarded him as indestructible. Blinded in the right eye in a fight in his younger days, he wore a greasy leather patch over the redundant milky ball. His left eye, however, was blue, piercing and all-seeing. On his day he could out-brag and out-talk any mountain man with his far-fetched stories and ramblings.

"Heeard 'bout ye run-in with Bug's Boys," he said, casting a one-eyed bead toward the dried scalps hanging from the pommel of Rimmer's saddle.

From gossip and stories legend is formed and distance was clearly no impediment to rumour.

"Seems like the coon ye rubbed out was some kill; Runs in Shadow . . . big headman. Most thought 'im nigh on invincible. Best watch ye back when ye ride out."

For once Rimmer said nothing as Troom walked away. Isaiah stared at Rimmer with a probing look of concern as if expecting some kind of reaction. Rimmer, however, remained silent and drew deeply on his pipe, his face impassive.

Trappers drank and gambled far into the night rendering sleep impossible. At around four in the morning a number of shots were fired amid roars, yells and raised voices. At dawn one man lay dead and another lay mortally wounded. He tossed, moaned and rambled for hours tended by his Indian wife before passing away the hour before dusk.

The following day more mountain men rode in; almost less than human wild men. Men who had forged a life in the wilderness for years. They were dressed in animal skins laced with rawhide thongs and furs, with braided hair and beards that hung to their thighs; some with ageing Indian women, all with pack mules loaded with beaver, otter, wolverine, and bear skins.

Some were armed with ancient weapons and some had lost touch with civilisation for so long that their spoken English was no more than monosyllabic. They were all more than fluent, however, in numerous native tongues.

At night endless yarns and anecdotes were spun round the campfires. Drunken insults were occasionally thrown resulting in smashed teeth, fractured jaws, noses and cheekbones.

The wild drunken raucousness, knife and fist fights, shooting contests, wrestling matches, and unceasing fornication continued for days.

The surrounding woodland and copses became a stinking latrine after days of grunting trappers and hunters emptied their bowels just after dawn.

Likewise at night the woodland glades became scenes of debauchery as liquored-up mountain men copulated and sometimes raped and brutalised Indian women.

Indeed, one evening Isaiah ventured into the bushes to relieve himself only to intrude upon a great bear of a mountain man thrusting into a scrawny, ageing Indian woman against a tree, with her skirt hitched high, her legs round him and her expression one of rank indifference.

The dregs from an upturned rum keg dripped onto the ground. Clouds of tobacco smoke mingled with smoke from the fire. Jacob Troom was in full flow, holding court amidst a group of men which included Rimmer and Isaiah.

"Ye heeard 'bout the so-called Death Spirit of the evenin' star; that's what some tribes call it south o' the Yellowstone. Indian girls bin found raped and butchered. Seems like any Indian girl wanderin' alone is likely prey. Heeard tell that it strikes at dusk. No coon's seen it, they say it vanishes like a spirit into the night."

Troom took a breath and drew deep on his long-stem clay pipe.

"Molar here's seen 'em."

Molar was young, an orphan and social misfit. He had come to the mountains to escape society. His sun-cooked face was ingrained with dirt. His brown hair hung lank and greasy and a wispy beard fuzzed his cheeks and chin. When he spoke he did so with a tilt of the head, perusing with one eye. His voice was surprisingly rich as he drew on his cob pipe.

"Come across two of 'em no more'an a quarter mile from Crazy Woman's. They was both young, no morn twelve, ide say. Both of 'em naked and strapped to a tree with thar throats cut. They were slash cut from chest ter belly in the shape of a fork, spikes down. Middle spike cut down straight to thar privits; the two side spikes curved out from the middle slash onto thar thighs. They was both squattin' in they own blood."

"Sounds like the Trishul!"

Pipes were removed, and inquisitive eyes were suddenly on Isaiah.

"It's the Devil's pitchfork; supposed to call down Satan so that he can collect Pagan souls and deliver them to Hell. That's if you believe in that kind of thing."

Grunts and murmurs followed as pipe stems were replaced between gnarled, pursed lips and weathered hair-veiled heads nodded. Troom's eye grew wide with fascination. Rimmer drew on his pipe and then spat into the fire.

"The Devil's shit! It's no more'an some fuckin' deranged fool on a butcherin' spree!"

Molar continued: "What's more ah reckon thar's more'an one o' them so-called death spirits; I recollect two sets o' tracks leadin' off from them corpsis."

More pipe smoke was blown from impassive, bearded faces, and there were more grunts and nodding of heads, and another keg of rum was passed round, and led by Troom the yarns continued into the night.

Rendezvous was reaching its final days and beginning to slowly disperse when a low wailing broke the rare silence of the penultimate dawn.

Ujarek was amongst the Crow Indians who had come to trade that Rendezvous. He had come for trade whisky and had passed away during the night.

Watseka ran to her father's tipi to find her stepmother stooped and moaning over Ujarek's waxy, bloated and ochre-tinged body. With scant remorse she closed his yellow eyes and wiped the blood-streaked vomit from his chest. She then wrapped him in a robe in readiness for his body to be transported by travois back to the Crow burial ground.

Below the delicate purple beauty of Aconitum, the Devil's Helmet lays its deadly poisonous root. Likewise concealed by the land's transient beauty is an underlying brutalism that is the threat of death. Set apart from men who lived city lives, Rimmer lived life on the edge in a honed mind-set that was charged with foreboding in an unforgiving wilderness, and in Isaiah's mind his destiny could only ever be played out in these mountains, and for him there could never be another life. And as they journeyed back to his cabin Rimmer made it clear that he had been more than satisfied with their partnership and the resulting remuneration from the weeks of toil, and after much consideration it was his intention to trap on for one more year and he would be obliged if Isaiah would continue in cahoots with him, to which Isaiah eagerly agreed.

13

The great lake of Yellowstone stretched serene and shimmering in the crystal heat of the Harvest Moon and in the distance lay the white-capped range of the Continental Divide.

On its shore Isaiah feasted on freshly caught spit-roast cutthroat trout. He was days from Rimmer's cabin and rich in time until he and Rimmer would trap again.

Isaiah was a loner and there were times when he sought solitude and embarked on lone rides; and there were times when he would be gone for many days.

After clearing the mountain passes he had ridden down through valleys of scattered lodgepole pine of rich Viridian and summer fragrance and then on to Yellowstone.

At dusk at the great lake the sky to the west became a slow, shifting blanket inferno of orange crimson and soft grey. From the lake he rode on over ice-formed lava beds of cracking sinter to a land of boiling, gurgling pools, of ethereal mists that drifted like ectoplasm, a land of loneliness that provoked deep thought and wonder. Hot springs of silica richness simmered and bubbled across desolate miles. Geysers erupted with powerful spurts of sulphuric steam, jetting white mists and scalding water high into the air.

The dawn light made its slow, insidious advance through the damp, humid, vaporous air of Yellowstone. Intermittent shots of sunlight lit the bubbling ground through steaming mist. A distant erupting geyser blasted its hot haze skyward.

There had been no sign of human life. For days Isaiah's solitude had been absolute. At night the low murmur of Yellowstone had occasionally been broken by the high-pitched call of a bull elk or the screech of a bald eagle high on a mountain peak.

Isaiah had camped on higher ground and was breakfasting on coffee and pemmican when a figure emerged from the mist that had enveloped distant clusters of pines. It approached slowly with the distorted gait of the cripple, lurching to one side with each step. A faint, dark, static glow appeared to outline its form against the mist-blurred viridian of the trees.

As it approached Isaiah identified it as an ancient. His hair was stark white and trailed the ground. He wore a long-fringed deerskin robe and walked with the aid of a crook. His eyes were black slits in a small, pinched, dark, creviced, hollow face.

His hair was woven with an assortment of tiny charms and dried animal parts.

He placed his crook on the ground and slowly and painfully sat cross-legged close to Isaiah. He remained silent for some time and then spoke in a frail voice in an obscure native tongue Isaiah was not familiar with, gesturing continually toward the north and fixing Isaiah through the slits that masked invisible eyes.

Isaiah poured him coffee and gave him pemmican. He broke the pemmican into small pieces and dropped them into the coffee until they softened. He then fished them out and chewed them with toothless gums. When he had finished he continued to mutter in his strange tongue and again pointed toward the north, this time touching Isaiah on the shoulder with his crook.

After a short while he slowly got to his feet, leaned on his crook and went on his way.

Isaiah watched him slowly hobbling into the distance until he finally seemed to be absorbed by the morning haze, and then for a short while Isaiah dwelt on the enigma of the old man of the mist and a nagging compulsion to cut short his wandering solitude and return to Rimmer's cabin suddenly gripped him.

After riding out of Yellowstone, the course of his journey did not take him back the way he had come and he found that he had veered west, following tracks that took him over high bluffs and winding, rocky escarpments.

After a day's ride he rode down through scrubland to a creek that fed a stream running north-west.

At the creek bottom rock formation had created a series of overhanging ledges of natural shelter and it was here that he made camp.

His pony drank deep of the clear water and again Isaiah made fire, boiled coffee and ate pemmican.

As dusk fell he lay back and gazed at the great glittering void of the black night and reflected once again on the appearance of the old man and endeavoured to wrestle significance from his gestures and his incoherent mumblings.

He woke just after dawn, relieved himself against the rockface and then drank a pint of creek water. He breakfasted on more pemmican, refilled his water sack, mounted his pony and continued his ride south-west.

He rode a rocky track up to a ridgeline that was backed by dense forests of Aspen and Juniper. The ridgeline provided a rocky but flat riding track that stretched for miles in the direction of Rimmer's cabin.

The high heat of summer began to build with the morning and it burned on Isaiah's back as he rode. Blowflies pestered his pony's eye matter.

The sky was cloudless and sank to a purple-tinged, shimmering horizon. High on the thermals a falcon plunged and took prey in mid-flight.

The village in the lower valley came into view as Isaiah rode a sharp curve in the ridgeline. It was large and appeared to stretch around a quarter of a mile along a stream that meandered the valley bottom. Sparkling sunlight lit the grey-brown and tawny white of the tipi hides. Lodge poles jutted high through smoke holes and the blue haze of cooking fires drifted skyward in the breezeless air. A low murmur of sound mixed with the shrieks of children's voices seemed to carry on the morning air. In the distance a huge pony herd grazed in a meadow of sap green. Women worked in groups along the banks of the stream. A bustle of tiny figures flecked with colour wove in and out amongst the lodges.

Steep slopes to the west of the village were thickly wooded and rose hundreds of feet to a rocky parapet, its skyline jagged against the brilliant morning light.

Isaiah pulled back and continued his ride amid the cover of trees that ran parallel to the ridgeline.

He rode on for around ten miles.

A dark form against a tree just under a quarter of

a mile distant caught his eye. As he rode closer his pony became skittish, its nostrils widening as it tossed its snorting head. Closer and the form became recognisable as human. Closer still and there, glaring, the Trishul screamed its vile and bloody message.

She was young, a child of no more than thirteen years, naked and lashed to a tree with rawhide thongs. The thongs had tightened with the morning heat and were constricting her dead flesh. Her head hung forward and her thick black hair shone in the light.

Nearby was her fringed deerskin dress and moccasins, the leather fastenings cut.

The ground below her was black with blood, just as Molar had described. The bloody Trishul had been slashed from throat to belly and then out in two curves down each thigh. The thick pale-edged flesh curled back from both sides of her wounds and swarmed with flies. Blood had oozed from her brutalised vagina and dried vertical rivulets ran down her body.

Scavengers had not yet done their work; she had not long been killed.

Isaiah dismounted and recoiling as he approached, he gently lifted her head. Serene in death, her eyelids were closed and her expression calm.

Throat bruising indicated that she had been

strangled before being mutilated. He cut for sign, and sure enough, just as Molar had described there was more than one set of tracks running north.

He cut the girl down and placed her body in a shallow gully and covered her with rocks. Then he rode on.

On his return Rimmer's response to Isaiah's account and description of the dead Indian girl was one of rank indifference and dismissiveness.

"Git yer mind on what's ahead, boy; thar's weapons ter clean and Galena ter pour, fresh meat's low, signs are fer a crool winter comin' and we need ter prepare. Then thar's trappin' agin come Pink Moon."

Indeed, for some time after Isaiah's return Rimmer had been uncharacteristically withdrawn and occasionally bad tempered, sometimes berating Watseka over nothing more than trivia.

And sure enough the ensuing winter was harsh compared to the previous year and throughout the grim freezing months Rimmer's moods fluctuated from tetchiness to bearable tolerance.

He frequently intimated that once and for all this would be his final year as a trapper and that after Rendezvous he intended to retire with Watseka to his cabin in Taos.

In his thoughts Isaiah attributed Rimmer's

moods to the anticipation of a life without challenges, of total change after thirty years in the mountains, and the adjustment he would be compelled to make. And there were times when he sensed that Rimmer was staring into an abyss of uncertainty.

Throughout the winter, in addition to hunting trips with Rimmer, Isaiah continued his lone excursions, sometimes on foot exploring tracks which led to higher levels and bitterly cold freezing peaks.

Meat fed, he was now hard and raw-boned. He wore his hair constantly braided, Crow-style. His skin was now sun-ravaged and Rimmer never ceased to be impressed by how impervious he was to any form of hardship, tolerating without complaint searing heat or lacerating cold and, not for the first time, muttering to himself, "Youth aint normal!"

14

With the arrival of the Pink Moon, and with it the great thaw, Rimmer and Isaiah made plans to set off once again to trap streams Rimmer's Crow informants had described as still beaver-rich; north-west toward the land of the Bloods.

Once again Watseka would be left with her Crow cousins until the summer Rendezvous.

Rimmer had always risen before dawn, however on the morning he and Isaiah had planned to leave he slept on, finally stirring an hour and a half after daybreak. He sat on the edge of the wooden bunkbed staring at the ground for some time. Watseka brought him coffee which he sipped, then fumbling with his tobacco pouch he lit his first pipe of the morning.

Isaiah stared at him as he drew deep on the stem

of his pipe and exhaled the smoke. He was ashen-faced, and for the first time Isaiah thought him old, older than he had ever appeared before.

"You alright, Josh? We can ride out in a day or so if yer like."

"No, I'm ready. We'll make tracks," Rimmer wheezed as he heaved himself from the bunk.

They rode out with the pack mules later that morning, and after leaving Watseka with her relatives, they rode north-west into a chill wind that still bore a hint of winter's dying breath.

All around the forests and woodland shimmered with the acid green of new growth and sprouting buds.

Rimmer rode uncharacteristically hunched in the saddle with his buffalo robe pulled tightly round his shoulders. He was strangely subdued and Isaiah sensed that perhaps all was not right.

After a day's ride Isaiah began to sense a fleeting presence, a sensation Rimmer's instincts would have usually picked up on. This time, however, Rimmer said nothing and kept riding. Isaiah constantly scanned the rock formations and woodland, but saw no one.

They rode on for a second day and in the early evening Rimmer chose a clearing by a stream backed by a low rock wall to make camp for the night.

Rimmer dismounted and with his robe

remaining round his shoulders, sank down against a tree. Isaiah began to prepare camp and make fire. Rimmer appeared weary and breathless, his ravaged face sallow and his eyes like slits in the fading light. He filled his pipe bowl and without lighting it, placed the stem between his lips. He mumbled something which to Isaiah was virtually inaudible and then began to stare vacantly down into the stream.

The calm of the early evening was suddenly shattered by the screech of a war cry as two warriors, faces black like demons, broke from the cover of the dense woodland on the far bank of the stream and charged across the shallow water.

With no time to pull a weapon Isaiah whipped round and took one of the warriors full on, parrying the angled blow of the warrior's hatchet handle with his left hand, the downward force splitting the webbing between his thumb and forefinger.

They grappled in a deadly embrace for some time before Isaiah managed to power a low blow with his fist into the warrior's gut, sending him stumbling back gasping for air. Isaiah then quickly pulled his Green River and charged the warrior. Both men then fell into the stream with Isaiah pinning the warrior under him, and with all his upper body strength slowly powered his knife down toward the warrior's chest. The warrior struggled bravely for his life in an attempt to force

Isaiah's arms upward. His wide, thin-lipped mouth gaped in a teeth-flashing grimace; black streaks glistened on his forehead and nose. Both men's faces almost touched as the warrior's black eyes bore into Isaiah.

Slowly the warrior's resistance began to weaken, and with all his weight Isaiah slowly pushed the blade through the warrior's ribs. He screamed a defiant war cry and then began to moan his death song.

As the blade made its way through fat and tissue into the warrior's lung, his eyes became inflamed with hatred, and then exhaling with a rasping sigh and spluttering blood, an ironic haze of ecstasy clouded his upward rolling pupils, and his lips parted in a grotesque smile, and the water in the stream ran red with his blood.

Meanwhile, the second warrior was onto Rimmer with breathtaking speed. His pipe fell from his lips as he glared upward at the porcupine-quilled demon silhouetted against the blue evening light.

Rimmer groped for the Collier, all too slow; his reflexes dulled by the mild stroke he had suffered in his sleep two nights previous. The Rimmer of old was no more.

The Pogamoggan came down in an arc, cleaving Rimmer's temple. His head jerked sideways, his eyes bulged and his tongue shot forward as he gasped in agony. Ferocious repeated blows to Rimmer's neck severed major arteries causing blood to jet onto the tree against which he was leaning.

As Isaiah eased himself up from the now inert body of the dead brave, a war cry that chilled the blood broke the silence, and pulling his knife from the warrior's chest, he turned to the vision of Rimmer's bloody scalp lock being held aloft in triumph. He then stared in disbelief at the bloodied, almost decapitated form of his slumped mentor.

The warrior then roared again in defiance, turned and darted back across the stream and then into the trees the way he had come. Isaiah gave chase but the warrior was lean and faster and made it back to his tethered pony. Then in a flash he was gone, his hoofbeats becoming less audible as he weaved through the sparse woodland.

Both warriors had left the Blackfeet village days before; their mission to avenge the killing of Runs in Shadow, the most venerated headman of his generation.

They had both sought the path of greatness by returning to their village with the scalp lock of his killer. One warrior had been triumphant, the other had lost his life.

Eager to get back to Rimmer, Isaiah did not give further chase. Leading the pony of the Indian he had killed, he made his way back to where Rimmer lay.

Rimmer's left temple had been bludgeoned in and his neck was partially severed. The ground beneath him was black with blood. He had died with his eyes open and even in death the penetration of his stare had not dimmed.

To Isaiah belief in Rimmer's invincibility had always been absolute and the sense of disbelief came in waves as he stared down at his mentor in death.

He closed Rimmer's eyes, placed a hand on the gnarled fists he had clenched in his final agony and muttered a final farewell. Often blunt, crude, sometimes insulting, always pragmatic, despite all his faults, Isaiah's loyalty to him had never wavered, and as he glanced back through the trees in the direction the remaining warrior had ridden, the sudden realisation came to him that others would surely come, others who would also seek the path of greatness, however next time they would be seeking him.

Isaiah laid Rimmer's body out and covered him with his robe. That evening he continued to churn his thoughts whilst sitting by a low flickering fire until dusk fell into night.

He thought of Watseka and how she would receive the news of Rimmer's passing.

Weariness finally took him and he fell into a disturbed sleep, waking occasionally from the drone of Rimmer's voice distorted by dreams and the night breeze in the trees. Sleep would then take him again, and then, after a while, he would wake expecting Rimmer to be snoring under his robe opposite the fading embers, and the bloody events of the previous day would again jar his consciousness.

The following morning he broke camp, packed all trapping accoutrements onto the mules, heaved Rimmer's body onto his pony, covered him with his robe and began the journey back to the Crow village.

Somehow sensing that his owner was now a burden in death, Rimmer's mount was unusually nervous, prancing and pulling on his halter.

After two days' ride through forest, waist-high grassed plains, and stalked by wolves sensing dead meat, at twilight Isaiah rode the copse-lined track that descended into the valley of the Crow village.

As he rode a running figure emerged at the end of the track in the fading light. As the figure approached he recognised it as Watseka. Acting on a compulsion driven by primal instinct she had sensed her husband's approach and from her father's lodge she had run to receive him at the end of his final ride.

Her face riven with anxiety she ran to Rimmer's pony and lifted the buffalo robe that covered his lifeless form. She ran her hand over his shoulder and back and laid her head on his thigh. Then she began to chant softly a whimpering lament.

As dusk fell they entered the Crow village and all the while Watseka continued her chant, never breaking contact with Rimmer's body.

Brief homage was paid by some men of the

village as they rode in. Isaiah carried Rimmer's body into the great tipi and laid him on a robe. Watseka knelt beside him and placing both hands on his chest she began to rock to and fro. Her chant then became a slow moan and finally a shrill, wrenching wail.

Anguish tore at Isaiah as he watched her swaying and rocking in her grief.

Her wailing continued intermittently for the remainder of the evening and then through the night.

As the lingering night drifted on and with the warmth from the lodge fire, weariness eventually took Isaiah, and in spite of Watseka's droning chant, fell into a deep sleep.

He woke in the early hours of the morning to the sight of Watseka slumped over Rimmer's body. Tear-diluted blood oozed from slashes on her forearms and ran in tiny rivulets through his lifeless fingers.

Exhaustion took her just after dawn and she fell unconscious over Rimmer's body. Isaiah lifted her onto a robe where she slept until dusk. When she woke she continued her grieving with a chant that was no more than a whimper. Preventing her from continuing to self-mutilate was a struggle, however being rendered weak through exhaustion, she did not resist and after running her hands once more over Rimmer she fell onto her robe and slept on.

She woke the following morning with a sense

that perhaps the force of her penance had been absolute, and that her emotional sacrifice should manifest itself in sorrow to a spirit guide and those who had gone before. It was time for her husband to begin his journey.

The odour of putrefaction had begun to taint the air of the lodge and that day two women of the village elders bound Rimmer's body with rawhide soaked in tallow.

Rimmer's attitude to all matters spiritual had always been summed up in one word: "Hokum." Rimmer was the ultimate pragmatist and gave credence only to what he saw and occasionally what he heard. Watseka, however, led her life according to the spiritual rituals and beliefs of her ancestors and it was her wish, that in spite of her husband's lack of reverence for Crow belief, he be laid to rest according to tradition on a scaffold on high ground, near his cabin, as close as possible to the sacred cosmos.

During the long winter evenings in the cabin Watseka had attempted to teach Isaiah the basic language of sign and after her grieving she struggled to communicate her beliefs to him. In sign she expressed that the spirit of a person never dies and that after death they begin a journey to a higher plain.

Rimmer must take his possessions on that journey and his pony must be sacrificed in order that he be carried safely there, and when he is laid to rest on his scaffold a sacred circle must be scribed on the ground around him and his dead pony laid within.

She also warned that his name must not be spoken out loud lest he may be called back from his journey.

And so on the morning after the day his body was bound, Rimmer was strapped to a travois and they began the trek through the lower passes back to Rimmer's cabin. Watseka rode the travois pony and remained silent and purposeful throughout the ride.

On reaching the cabin they then rode the high ground west for around a quarter of a mile through forest glades until they came to a grove that led to a clearing. Here Watseka nodded in approval indicating that this was the place.

Through forest vistas the western range lay serene in clear light, and above, framed by foliage, the infinity of the sacred cosmos indicated the "way", the course of Rimmer's spirit journey.

From the surrounding woodland Isaiah cut ten lodgepole limbs approximately eight feet long.

At the clearing Watseka had chosen, he staked four deep into the forest earth on a rectangular format measuring around five feet by eight feet.

At the top, at both ends across the shorter lengths, he lashed on two cross members with hide thongs. He then laid and lashed the remaining limbs on at intervals, bridging the two end spans to create a platform.

He and Watseka then lifted and laid Rimmer's bound body onto the scaffold. Watseka wrapped his Hawken rifle, his Green River and his pipe in a hide bundle and placed them next to his body. The scalps he had taken, which included the hair of the Blackfeet headman Runs in Shadow, were tied to each corner.

Then chanting breathlessly she scribed the sacred circle into the soft earth to encompass the scaffold.

Finally she led Rimmer's pony into the circle and whispering and breathing gently into his nostrils, he submitted to her and she coaxed him onto his side.

In a flash the blade was in his neck and his blood pulsed onto the leaf-mouldered ground. He shuddered and spasmed briefly before his wide eyes clouded and he drifted away.

For a while they both sat cross-legged on the ground and gazed up at Rimmer's body. A sudden strengthening breeze from the west lifted the scalps and they began to dance and flutter like the wings of a crow.

Watseka whimpered from deep in her throat and raised her arms to him, and then a sense of departure breathed its poignancy through forest glades and into infinite space, and then she knew that Rimmer had finally gone.

Back at the cabin Watseka took to the bunk that she had always shared with Rimmer and slept.

Isaiah became uneasy with ambivalent feelings of expectation and doubt, finding himself alone with the woman who had obsessed his thoughts under Rimmer's gaze for over two years, and again he chopped logs in an effort to work off the adrenalin that coursed his body.

The remainder of the day he spent in deep thought, recording the events that had surrounded his mentor's death in his journal.

Watseka did not emerge until the following morning when at dawn Isaiah found her laying a fire and boiling coffee.

They breakfasted on coffee and pemmican in silence, their eyes barely making contact.

After some time in which they did not communicate Watseka disappeared into the bunk room and returned with an oak strong box and placed it in front of Isaiah.

The wood was dark with age and its hasp and iron strap hinges were pitted with rust.

Isaiah lifted the lid and item by item removed the box's contents.

There was a roll of dollar bills, Rimmer's share of their pelt takings; a silver locket containing a lock of grey hair, and on the back was engraved: "To C, all love. W"; a collection of cob and clay pipes; a bone-handled Bowie knife in a hide-fringed and beaded sheath; a teak case containing a fine pair of flintlock pistols with polished walnut stocks inlaid with silver fretwork made by a London gunsmith; a piece of rolled, yellowed parchment on which were inscribed the land deeds to Rimmer's cabin in Taos; and finally a sheet of rolled buckskin tied round with a rawhide thong.

Isaiah untied the thong and unrolled the thin leather sheet. On it, scrawled in a clumsy hand in what appeared to be charcoal, was the following:

Last will n testimint of Joshua Fredrick Rimmer.

Ah leave all that ah own ter Izia Stina and that incloods ma spous Watseka. Son, if ye read this, ah no ye have feelins for her, they weren't sa hard ter pick up and ah no ye'll treet er good.

Son, ah thank ye for yer loyilty and yer cumridship. It was a plesha ter trap with ye and fite alongsid ye.

Sined this day of the Hunta's Moon 1831, Joshua Rimmer.

Watseka sat cross-legged staring at him as he replaced the objects back into the box. He sat in front of her, lifted her hand, and then with considerable apprehension endeavoured to communicate Rimmer's last wishes to her.

Had she understood? Isaiah pondered.

Finally she got to her feet, remained expressionless and returned to the bunk room where she remained for the entire day.

His answer came that night when he woke to her

dark form above him, silhouetted against the moonlight.

The light modulated her shoulders and the pure curve of her hips; it touched her black hair and it kissed her powerful features. She lifted his robe and laid against him, then ran her cool fingers gently over his cheeks, lips and forehead.

Her hair lightly brushed his shoulders as her lips parted and with the light now clear on her face the abyss of her black eyes seemed to hold a parody of both pleasure and foreboding. She gasped as he clutched her to him, then realising the power of his embrace he released her. The man in him reared hard and eager with her caresses. Her fragrance was indefinable; mint, wild thyme, the swaying grasses of the plains, all toyed with his senses. His head spun from her primal breath and the taste of her saliva.

Her dark, fine-grained skin of rich lustre glinted in the low light as he tenderly explored the silkiness of her secret lips. His thick beard lightly brushed her skin as he kissed her breasts.

Her legs parted and then he rolled between them. She caught her breath as he entered her. She panted and writhed under him as he thrust gently. The moment was short-lived; within minutes she groaned in her orgasm clawing at his shoulders as he climaxed with her.

Then he tasted the salt of her tears, felt her

breath on his cheek and neck as she whispered a low murmur in Crow.

Sleep then took them both in the clear, humid night.

With the dawn came oppressive skies and thunder reverberated through the peaks and the forest glades, and as the roar of torrential rain lashed the cabin he took her again, and after what seemed timeless love-making her orgasms became multiple; tugging at his shoulder-length hair as she arched her back and stiffened her toes in her groan of ecstasy.

With late morning the storm abated and the oppressive veil of yellow-grey crept slowly toward the horizon leaving a sparkling azure brilliance in its wake.

Crystal droplets glistened in the sunlight as they fell from foliage and the astringent air was intoxicating with its damp fragrance.

He carried her naked to the waterfall and its icy spray took their breath, and such was the power of his unabated desire that he embraced her repeatedly under the roaring force of the fall.

Back at the cabin Watseka wrapped herself in a blanket and began to lay logs and kindling for a fire. Meanwhile Isaiah returned to his bunk, only to be met by the stunning revelation of his mentor's impotency glaring at him from the bloody stain of a broken hymen on the robe on which he and

Watseka had made love; Rimmer's marriage to her had never been consummated.

By the fire Watseka sipped water and Isaiah drank the hot coffee she had made. He gazed at her in silence. Her damp hair clung to her shoulders and streaked her hard, erect nipples, and transfixed and pulsed with desire he took her yet again. Through the hours of the afternoon until dusk they laid in a caress-filled embrace, and when darkness fell, exhaustion and sleep finally took them both.

15

By September, the Moon of Harvest, Watseka's body had taken on a new fullness, her skin a delicate translucency, her belly swollen, and the surging chemistry within her was palpable; and she was clear in her desire to winter in the Crow village and there marry Isaiah according to Crow custom.

A sharp easterly breeze marked the beginning of October, the Hunter's Moon, as they rode an incline through a rock-strewn mountain pass that led to a forest track that finally broke out into the flat meadows through which the Shoshone River ran.

The great village meandered the snaking river valley for one and a half miles. In both directions either side of the river the land rose in thickets of cottonwood, elder and lodgepole pine, providing the village with a natural shield to the blizzards that swept from the north-east.

Shrouded in sterile cold, bitter mists and forever drifting woodsmoke, the inevitable cycle of the seasons saw the village endure yet another interminable winter. Clad in hides, fur side in, the women melted chunks of ice in iron kettles over fires to obtain drinking water.

Tiama was a hermaphrodite and a deaf mute who many years previous was discovered as a child, semi-mutilated and abandoned in a cave, by a lone Crow hunter. Although predominantly female, she also possessed a semblance of male genitals. From whence she had come and who had sired her remained a mystery, and her story had become legend.

Raised by Crow women, Tiama was considered a sacred being, and throughout the winter Isaiah rode out with hunting parties in which her presence was revered. She was the equal of many men as a hunter and had ridden in raiding parties and killed with brutal efficiency.

Her strange scarred features appeared to modulate according to angle and the play of light. Tall and strong with light brown hair cropped to the neck, and with gold beaded rings in her ears, her presence was both striking and formidable.

She lived alone in a tipi on the edge of the village away from the main clusters of lodges, and it was forbidden for any warrior to attempt to lay with her, and those who had tried had been cast out from Crow society; and Watseka warned Isaiah of any kind of association with her.

Isaiah had been living with Watseka in the lodge of her late father and it was in the Snow Moon of February on an overcast morning with the sky heavy with snow that they rode in; two men, one heavily bearded with loose shoulder-length hair dressed in furs, the other a half-breed. They had come to trade with the Crow, rode mules, and in tow they led pack mules loaded with old muskets, powder, axes, hatchets and coffee beans.

Clad in a long hide coat and with waist-length braids, Briar pipe drooping from his lower lip, Hawken rifle in the crook of his arm, and Rimmer's Collier hanging from his belt, Isaiah emerged from Watseka's lodge and strode to his tethered pony. At the same time both men dismounted and began to make their way toward the centre of the village. They came to a halt when Isaiah caught their eye. Both men were familiar to him and both nodded in recognition. One was Joe Latife whom he remembered from Troom's campfire at Rendezvous. The other was the half-breed that had ridden past him and Rimmer on his first visit to the Crow camp. Latife had a reputation for cruelty, and it had been widely rumoured that he had beaten three of his Indian wives to death.

Latife squinted as he sized Isaiah up.

"Rimmer's boy aint ye?"

Isaiah drew on his pipe and nodded.

"Aint seen Josh for nigh on a year; recollect he weren't at last Rondivoo."

"Rimmer's dead!"

Latife jerked his head up in sudden reaction.

"Bug's boys, stone war club pretty much cleaved Josh's head in two."

Isaiah tensed inwardly as the memory momentarily flashed back.

"How many?" enquired Latife.

"Two of 'em, the one that did for Rimmer got away with his scalp."

"Ye do for th'other coon?"

Isaiah nodded and then blew out a cloud of tobacco smoke.

"Rimmer gone under! Never thought I'd hear the day," exclaimed Latife.

"Josh wasn't himself that day, never seen him so slow. I reckon he must have been ailing from something."

The breed looked dangerous as he scanned Isaiah with his yellow-green eyes.

"Bin livin' with the Crow, hev yer?"

"All winter," replied Isaiah.

Latife then nodded toward the Collier which was just visible under Isaiah's loose coat.

"That Rimmer's side arm ye warin'?"

"Yep! Left me all he owned."

"Took his woman ah seen." Latife nodded toward the tipi as Watseka emerged from the flap carrying strips of meat for drying. She was nearing her time and walked with a backward-leaning, lumbering gait, her belly huge.

Isaiah drew deep and then exhaled more tobacco smoke toward Latife and nodded.

"Ye surely struck gold thar, boy. Had ma eye on her for years; finest piece of squaw meat ah ever did see, and ah cin see from her belly ye bin stuffin' her real good," Latife drawled.

The remark sparked a surge of fury within Isaiah, and tossing the Hawken to the ground he went for Latife's throat, grabbed a fistful of hair, yanked his head forward, and then quietly, in Latife's ear, he rasped, "Soon that woman will become my wife, and I will have no man badmouthing her."

Latife began to splutter as Isaiah clamped his throat tighter. The breed then drew his knife as Isaiah released his grip and pushed Latife away. Both men then backed off as Isaiah quickly pulled the Collier.

Latife's eyes were black with anger as he backed away.

"Ye need ter watch ye temper, boy. Aint never knowed a Hiverano defend a damn squaw like that afore," he growled. "Thar'll come a time when you'd wished you'd never done that. Be wise ter watch yer back, boy." And with that he shoved the breed forward, muttered something in an Indian tongue, remounted and continued on toward the centre of the village.

Isaiah watched them for some time as they rode off, and picking up his Hawken, he became aware of Watseka staring at him stony-faced, and in that moment he read her thoughts. His move on Latife had been a bad one, and he began to regret his loss of control, and walking to his pony he became dogged by apprehension.

Towards the end of the Snow Moon, at the hour before dawn, Watseka went into labour. Isaiah was not permitted to remain with her.

An old woman entered the lodge carrying two wide stumps of grey elder roughly a foot and a half long. She placed them on the ground around three feet apart, a short distance from the lodge fire.

Watseka bore her labour well; she was in prime physical condition, and her ample buttocks and strong thighs were conducive to giving easy childbirth.

After the sun had risen to illuminate a hoar

frost-covered land, Watseka supported herself on the two stumps and squatted between them, and straining hard and with a low moan, a tiny, steaming, bloodied head began to appear. It exuded slowly from between her legs, and with her eyes screwed she strained once more, and with perspiration dripping from her, the remainder of the miniature body slithered gently onto the warmed ground.

The old woman did not touch the child as it emerged; it was a given that a child's first contact with the world must be the sacred ground.

The infant's cry was both piercing and resonant as the old woman cut and knotted the umbilical cord and bathed the child in sweet, tepid spring water.

Watseka, calm and unflustered, then wiped the blood and mucous of birth from her inner thighs and lay back exhausted on a robe in front of the fire.

The old woman wrapped the child, a girl, in a blanket and placed it in Watseka's arms. Her tiny head quivered as she strived for her mother's breast, and then she suckled eagerly.

Sometime after Isaiah was allowed back into the lodge to meet his infant daughter. Transfixed he took her gently in his arms. She stared up at him with Crow black eyes. Her complexion was swarthy and deep, and her black hair touched with glints of light. She squirmed against his chest whimpering and striving once again for the nipple.

And so by the power of her lungs when bathed in the sweet water, they named her Wanoka.

Through the woodsmoke haze of a Crow evening on the cusp of dusk, late in the Worm Moon of March, Isaiah and Watseka married according to the custom of the Blanket ceremony.

Watseka was bound in a blanket that had been adorned with beaded horizontal lines, each representing stages in her life. Then to an ancient chant she began to move at a slow walking rhythm.

In the glow of a dozen fires she transfixed Isaiah's gaze and after almost an hour of gestural movement she allowed the blanket to fall to the ground to reveal the cream-grey of her fringed elkskin robe decorated with porcupine quills and fine beadwork. Her loose calf-length hair swayed in the orange light as she turned and beckoned to him. He joined her close and moved slowly with her.

A second blanket of pure white was then wrapped round them both to bind them in marriage and to symbolise union. And later that evening they celebrated into the night feasting on elk steaks, boudins and fox boiled in blood, water, sassafras and wild rosemary.

Leaving Watseka and Wanoka with their Crow

cousins, and driven by a compulsion rooted in Rimmer's mentoring and memory, Isaiah became a lone trapper that spring, plying the trade in dangerous country.

Beaver had been scarce that season and after weeks in the wilderness his plew tally had been disappointing, and so as spring began to blossom into early summer, he made preparations for the trek back to his wife and daughter.

He had hobbled his pack mules in a secluded gully some distance from the stream and his camp. The gully widened into a track that led into a small canyon, and as he was securing pelts to his pack mules, a distant rider emerged from a copse and came into view, riding at a steady lope down the track.

As the rider came closer it became clear that it was a Blackfeet warrior. Foolishly Isaiah had left his Hawken and the Collier at his camp a short distance from the stream and he found himself armed only with his Green River.

The rider came to a halt around forty feet away. He was naked but for breach clout and knee-length moccasins strapped with red thongs. His skin was dark and his body lean and wiry. Lighter ribs of battle scars ran across his chest and upper thighs. His top knot was bound with silver wire, and black and tawny stripes ran in rivulets down his cheeks and forehead.

He coaxed his pony into repeated prancing circles and at the same time yelled a rasping challenge to Isaiah, then with superb horsemanship, galloped like lightning towards him and as he passed lashed him across the face with a braided leather quirt, and then galloped away, only to turn and charge once again.

The charges then came one after another, faster and faster, lashing Isaiah each time until his head spun and bled with the speed and pain of the whipping.

After the sixth charge, with acute timing, Isaiah managed to grab the quirt and wrench the rider from his pony, and as the warrior stumbled to the ground he rolled over at speed, regained his balance in seconds and drew a knife. He then came at Isaiah like lightning, his blade glinting in the late morning sun. Isaiah managed to pull his own Green River, but only after the first slash from the warrior had ploughed downwards into Isaiah's chest drawing blood.

The warrior was fast and nimble and the pace of his attack threatened to overwhelm Isaiah, and he began to duck and weave in order to avoid the blur of the blade. Another slash caught Isaiah on the forearm again drawing blood. The warrior kept coming like a whirlwind and in desperation Isaiah lunged low, diving at the warrior's feet, and at the same time stabbing into his calf. Blood jetted from a femoral vein as he danced back with a yell and crouched to the ground. The warrior's defences were then momentarily down and Isaiah seized his chance, springing forward, and with the force of momentum, rammed his blade into the warrior's neck. The warrior's knife then slipped from his grasp, and with a gurgling moan, clutched at his neck as blood spurted in intermittent jets into the air and over Isaiah's chest. For a few seconds the warrior struggled and squirmed as life quickly ebbed from him, until he finally fell back and lay inert on the rocky ground.

Isaiah's wounds were only surface slashes, however they bled profusely, and returning to his camp he bathed them in the stream, stitched them with catgut and bound them with strips of calico; and with the sun still high made his way to the dead warrior.

Then lifting the warrior's neck ran his blade round the top of the warrior's head cutting to the bone; then placing one foot on the man's shoulder, grabbed his streaked hair with both hands and wrenched it free. Blood oozed down over the warrior's forehead as Isaiah's first trophy came away with a sucking sound that echoed through the narrow canyon.

It was mid-June when Isaiah rode into the Crow

village with his pack mule only half-laden, and the scalp of a would-be assailant swaying from the pommel of his saddle. Rendezvous would be at Green River again that year and he intended to be there in this July of the Buck Moon.

16

> The earth we tread is sacred. We the Crow have made this land; we the Crow have become this land.
>
> – Thoughts of a holy man.

It was the time that the Shaman sensed voices from a dimension steeped in the souls of his ancestors that drifted from the annals of incalculable time, asking for renewal and sacrifice.

The heat of the Strawberry Moon parched and turned yellow the high grasses of the plains and transformed the quagmire that ran through the centre of the Crow village into a dust track where tiny twisters swirled and danced when whipped up by the wind; and on a morning late in June, when a hot wind blew from the south-west, young men including Isaiah were preparing for the Sun Dance.

Their bodies naked but for a breechclout were smeared with a mixture of white clay and buffalo tallow.

A tall pole was driven into the ground in the centre of the village, and from the top hung long, numerous strands of sinew.

The elders sat facing the arc of the sun's east-west meridian. The Shaman began the ritual of passing the pipe among them and then prayers from the pipe were offered to the four directions as well as the earth and sky; and when the sun reached its highest point in the azure brilliance and its rasp seared down on the dry encrusted ground, the drums began their incessant mesmeric pounding, breaking the hot sultry silence.

Each clay-encrusted warrior was tied at the waist to one of the lengths of sinew and began slow circular movements round the pole in unison with the beat of the drums.

As the dance progressed through the day, the clay on the warriors' skins began to crack and flake only to be moistened again from profuse perspiration.

Dusk fell and the dance continued into the night,

and then the bobbing, strand-restricted bodies took on demon-like visages as the orange light from the circle of fires illuminated their torsos. Some warriors fell exhausted, breaking the strands of sinew. Others danced on including Isaiah.

As night progressed the dance reached a sacrificial phase as heat exhaustion and thirst racked the circular moving bodies. Some cried out as they reached the mesmeric plain of trance.

Isaiah continued to move as the intermittent rhythm of the drums began to merge into an inaudible roar, and with it the slow ebbing away of dehydrated pain through soft dragging whispers, and then drifting, drifting to an elevated quasi-reality of a vision entrenched in visceral depths of subconsciousness.

A dark plain stretched to a distant horizon. Streaks of searing light illuminated a figure of a woman moving at a slow lope towards the light. He called to her and then began to run toward her. No matter how fast he ran, the distance between them remained constantly undiminished. He called to her once more, his voice reverberating in unison with the shimmering plain. She did not turn, her dark form loped on and on continually diminishing. Then the sudden clatter of fluttering wings as they brushed his shoulders, and then the sky darkened, and then blackness prevailed.

As his vision alternated between blur and focus

the coppery taste of his furred tongue eased as Watseka trickled water between his white, scum-rimmed lips.

He had endured the Sun Dance until late into the night when he collapsed and lost consciousness.

At dawn the drums silenced and Watseka's oval-shaped face framed dark hovered above him. He had given of his inner spirit through endurance and suffering and the elders praised the power it would transpose.

His vision remained clear in his consciousness and he described it to Watseka, who in turn referred to the Shaman in order to decipher its meaning.

Sitting cross-legged and staring directly into the sun, the Shaman remained silent for some time. Then in a voice that was barely audible he declared that Watseka's spirit hawk had returned briefly and that Isaiah had been infected by its force, and that his vision showed the remaining path he would travel in life, and that there would be a time in which its direction and his destiny would be unclear; after which he said no more.

The Shaman's words were laced with ambiguity, however there was no doubting the power of her husband's vision, and thereafter Watseka was beset with feelings of uncertainty.

In July Isaiah journeyed alone with his meagre pelt

tally to Green River for Rendezvous, leaving Watseka and the six-week-old Wanoka with their Crow cousins; and on his return he intended once again to winter with the Crow before travelling in early spring with his family to Rimmer's cabin to prepare for trapping that year.

On his journey to Rendezvous, in a mountain pass, another lone young Blackfeet warrior lost his life attempting to take him. This time there was no hand-to-hand struggle to the death; the warrior's charge ended swiftly with two shots from the Collier, one taking the warrior through the lung, and the other through the abdomen, and even before the warrior had taken his final groaning breath, Isaiah took his trophy.

One year and two months later in November, the Moon of the Beaver, Watseka gave birth to a second child, this time a boy. The child was large and in spite of her strength, her time in labour had been excruciating and the pain and struggle through the child's delivery had left her bleeding and exhausted.

The newborn's cry was strong and his tiny arms and legs punched the air, as the old birth mother washed the blood and slime of birth from his body. Watseka flinched as he clamped his tiny mouth with unusual force onto her nipple.

The healing of Watseka's birth traumas took

longer than anticipated and at times Isaiah became racked with anxiety over her wellbeing. The Shaman's potions, however, worked a slow recovery, and there were signs that her strength was returning when the milder winds began to temper the raw cold of a lingering winter.

Watseka's second child's complexion was dark, even for a Crow, and the soft down of his hair was raven black, and so in time she called him Little Dark.

It was early March, the beginning of the Moon of the Worm, and with his family Isaiah had made his yearly trek to Rimmer's cabin to prepare yet again for a way of life that was becoming increasingly precarious. The demand for beaver pelts had fallen away and the trade was entering its final death throes.

In the mountains many streams and rivers that were once rich in beaver had become "trapped out", and the animal was becoming increasingly scarce.

Soon Isaiah would be faced with a dilemma forced on him by circumstances. He could continue living with the Crow; this, however, was an imponderable that was fraught with foreboding. He had heard rumours at the last Rendezvous that there were notions and omens sensed by tribal prophets and holy men that in generations to come relentless forces from the east would deliver starvation, destruction and ultimate oblivion to the tribes of the upper Missouri.

He contemplated starting a new life in Rimmer's other adobe cabin in Taos. Through the sale of his pelts over the years, together with what he had inherited from Rimmer, he had accumulated a sizeable nest egg of American dollars.

However, here again he thought was an imponderable: How would he sustain his family when the money ran out and could Watseka adapt to life in relative civilisation?

Rendezvous of that year was a sad and depleted affair. With the fur trade in terminal decline the price he received for his pelts was a fraction of what his remuneration had been in previous years.

That year fewer trappers and hunters made their trek to the annual gathering, and it did not live up to the wild, debauched, drunken affairs of old.

Many of the seasoned Hiveranos of Rimmer's generation had gone; some had perished, some had drifted away from the mountains, and some had enlisted as army scouts. Even old Jacob Troom had finally met his end, savaged by a cougar somewhere in the high peaks.

Joe Latife and his half-breed companion were conspicuous around what evening campfires there were. Latife threw the occasional bitter glance at Isaiah, however no words were exchanged between the two men. Eventually Latife and the breed rode out as the final Rendezvous began to break up.

17

The time was early April, the Pink Moon and westerly winds had brought a gradual end to a great thaw, and the mountain air at Rimmer's cabin was charged once again with the stirrings of new life.

At four years Wanoka had grown tall for her age. She was lithe, wiry and constantly charged with boundless energy. Her dark eyes at birth had lightened and appeared to modulate in changing light. The honeyed bronze complexion so striking at birth had begun to fade. Her expressions were darting, she smiled constantly, her responses were sharp, and her energy infectious. And there were times when Isaiah would hum the laments of his youth, and then with her tiny voice she would pick them up almost pitch perfect. And when she ran and the sun caught glints in her hair, her doeskin frock would sway; and with each passing day he would admire her more and more.

By contrast the two-year-old Little Dark was a stocky child with strong limbs and an enormous appetite. He was a bright, blundering toddler and did not possess the nimbleness of his sister, although he did possess a kind of stoicism beyond his years, and seldom cried, and there were also times when he would chuckle fit to burst.

The morning was overcast; patches of cloud began to thin with a yellow glow as the sun began to burn through.

To Isaiah, Watseka appeared more comely than ever with her streaked hair stroking the packed earth floor as she knelt to lay a fire and boil coffee.

Wanoka and Little Dark played and squabbled in the coral at the side of the cabin.

Isaiah had slept well that night, however on waking he felt liverish and craved breakfast. Watching Watseka he continued to contemplate the future, and as a result became dogged by an uneasiness, a lingering anxiety that would churn within him in waves.

He breakfasted on buffalo jerky, moist with fat and pungent with wild rosemary, washed down with a pint of coffee and two pints of mountain water.

In order to satisfy his constant need for fresh

roasted meat, he intended that morning to ride down to the valley bottom to inspect a line of snares he had laid the day before.

He waved Watseka away when she attempted to braid his hair. He had the notion that morning that it should hang loose to his waist. Strands draped his chest and mingled with his fair beard which now touched his ribs. He wore a wolf's head cap and a trade blanket over his elkskin shirt belted at the waist. His fur-lined tallowed moccasins were bound with hide straps that ran up to the calf over buckskin leggings black with grease.

He carried his razor-honed Green River sheathed on his left hip with a hatchet on his right; and with his Hawken in the crook of his left arm, began the descent on one of his pack mules down the rocky track that led to the valley bottom.

He would be gone no more than a few hours.

The air was crisp and pungent with an earthy fragrance. Veils of mist hung in motionless suspension over the dense ranges of Aspen, Juniper and Blue Spruce. A jackrabbit darted across the track only to be lost in the undergrowth.

The mule snorted as its hooves crunched on the rocky inclines. The cloud cleared occasionally to allow intermittent bursts of sunlight to shimmer on moist leaves. The track widened as it levelled out through bushes and then into the dense leaf-mould-packed ground of the forest bottom.

He had laid a line of snares over a distance of roughly a quarter of a mile and he intended to inspect each one. He rode through wooded copses until he came to the edge of a glade where he had laid the first snare.

The Snowshoe Hare was a large male and squirming in the trap licking its bloody hind leg in an attempt to free itself. Isaiah slit its throat, released the snare and hung the kill over the mule's neck and rode on. The next two snares were without a kill. The final snare had trapped a squirrel which lay dead.

It was several hours before Isaiah returned to the bushy clearing that led to the track back to the cabin. He contemplated his meagre haul of kills as he urged the mule up the steep, rocky ascent.

Some distance from the top of the track his nostrils flared; "pony dung". He tethered his mule and continued on foot. Through a gap in the foliage in a glade he caught sight of three Indian ponies hobbled to saplings, a pile of fresh shit steamed by the hind legs of the nearest. He continued toward the cabin under cover of trees and heavy undergrowth.

A figure with shoulder-length, lank brown hair wearing a soiled wool jacket belted at the waist with a bone-handled sheathed knife on the left hip, and heavily-worn buckskin breeches, holding a rifle, stood in the cabin coral staring down into the valley below. The figure turned so that his profile became visible; he wore a gold ring in his right lobe and what appeared to be an elk tooth neckpiece.

Bile surged in Isaiah's gullet as his pulse began to quicken; it was the Breed.

A low, sinking, stomach-churning surge of foreboding quickly transmuted into simmering rage and hatchet drawn, he broke from cover and charged. The Breed attempted to turn and level his rifle, all too slow. Isaiah was on him, cleaving the Breed's neck with a scything, angled blow. Stumbling back with blood spurting from severed arteries, and cut through to cervical vertebrae the man's head flopped sideways attached only by sinew and skin. The air turned putrid with the odour of his evacuating bowels as Isaiah cleaved the Breed's head clean off with a second blow.

Now with saliva turned sour with dread and his neck crawling with demented anger he burst into the cabin to be met by a sight that blew his world into oblivion.

The bloodied, mutilated form of Little Dark lay draped across the rim of the great iron kettle in which Watseka had stewed venison. In death his tiny face was frozen in twisted agony.

There were sounds from the bunk room, and then a voice.

"C'mon, Joe, we aint got much tarm. Come ye load, ah aim ter git ma fill."

Isaiah tore through the rough-hewn door, Hawken primed and cocked. The room was rank with sweat and the testosterone of debauchery.

Watseka lay semi-conscious on the dirt floor, badly beaten and with blood oozing from a wound in her chest. With her deerskin dress hitched up to her waist and her legs spread wide, Joe Latife was raping her, grunting and moaning with the rise and fall of his stinking rump, the buckle of his belt rhythmically tapping on the dirt floor.

A frontier ruffian dressed in skins and wearing an eye patch stood with his boot on Watseka's shoulder and his hand on the butt of a pistol tucked into his belt.

The rasping cracked throat roar from Isaiah reverberated through the room as the man, wide-eyed, twisted, stepped back and attempted to pull the pistol.

The discharge from the Hawken blew the man's bowels inwards and sprayed blood and intestines against the wall of the cabin. With his abdomen smouldering the man groaned, staggered back and slumped to the floor, his body in a tremor.

Latife was slow to extricate himself from his pleasuring, and pulling away from Watseka made a fumbling attempt to pull up his breeches. Tossing the Hawken to the floor Isaiah pulled his Green River and with one slash severed Latife's half-erect penis. Latife screamed and tried to cap the spurting blood from the stump that remained.

Now in a frenzy Isaiah clubbed Latife to the ground and then stabbed him repeatedly in the chest and abdomen. A surge of revulsion then seemed to dampen his fury and he finally pushed himself up and stood for a few seconds gazing breathlessly at the bloody mass that was Latife's body.

He then turned and knelt by Watseka. He gently raised her head and stroked her cheek. Her breathing was shallow and erratic. He cut away her deerskin dress and pressed a blanket to her wound in an attempt to staunch the seepage of blood.

"Stay, stay with me," he whispered softly to her in Crow, then trembling he cradled her and gently rocked to and fro.

She murmured faintly and her breathing seemed to quicken.

He touched her lips and they parted and she struggled with her words. She appeared to rally and her tear-flooded eyes seemed to brighten and his hopes lifted.

He pulled her closer muttering and repeating softly, "Stay with me, stay with me".

Then her breathing became faint once more and the glint in her black eyes began to fade, and a strange and immediate wash of sallowness veiled her features. Then finally a surge of blood-streaked mucous rattled up from her chest and bubbled through her lips, and with a deep interminable sigh her chest sunk, and she drifted from him.

A grief-driven roar from Isaiah reverberated through the cabin once again as he clutched the lifeless Watseka to him, swaying to and fro.

He stayed with her for some time beset with guilt and self-loathing and racked by a simmering fury. If only he had not left her earlier that day. He wrestled with the thought over and over in his mind, and then despair gave rise to irrational notions and he toyed with ideas of joining her in death. Life would be unthinkable without her. Surely a dark void of despair lay ahead.

He then glanced through the open doorway toward the great stone fireplace, and there they were laying on the edge of the hearth, two tiny dolls made of twigs and twine; Wanoka, where was Wanoka?

Thoughts that she may be alive momentarily lifted his spirits.

He searched the outhouse, coral, surrounding bushes, rocky ground and copses. There were two sets of tracks running north from the glade where the murderers' ponies were tethered. The morning cloud cover had given way to clear, bright sunlight, and the glint of a tiny red bead on the trampled ground gave rise to hope.

Wanoka had been taken and thoughts that she may be alive gave rise to a locked mind-set. Driven by revenge he would be relentless whatever the terrain; night and day he would track her captors down, kill them and recover his daughter. All else was insignificant. This would be his mission and in the space of a morning the fat of time had grown lean.

Back at the cabin and choking with remorse he removed Watseka's blood-stained deerskin robe and dressed her in the beaded doeskin frock that she had worn when he married her.

He lay her on a buffalo robe and placed the tiny body of Little Dark in her arms. He then lay her meagre possessions by her side; her wooden-framed trade mirror, her tortoiseshell comb, her bone needles and her skinning knife. He stood and gazed at them both in death and searched for serenity in Watseka's features, but found none.

He cut a strand of her hair and tucked it into the corner pocket of his leather-bound journal, then wrapped the buffalo robe round them both and lashed it tight with rawhide thongs.

Then he gathered together his weapons, powder, lead, winter moccasins, buffalo robe coat, water sack and pemmican, and the roll of dollar bills he had accumulated over the years.

Into saddlebags also went Wanoka's dresses, moccasins and fur-lined cloak.

He heaved the bound bodies of his wife and son onto a pack mule and took one final look at

Rimmer's cabin. He had experienced ecstasy and peace there and now with the irony of fate's cruel cry he had experienced loss the like of which he had never known. He would never return and he would trap no more.

He scalped the three men he had killed and hung the dripping caps of skin and hair on the door of the cabin. Legend would record the bloodletting here. Then he dragged the corpses of the men into the coral, packed twigs and dry tinder round them, and striking flint, set them to smoulder.

With the pack mule and Watseka's pony in tow he headed for the glade where the remains of Rimmer lay.

The burial platform loomed stark and desolate as billowing rain clouds blew in from the north-west with a cutting wind. Rimmer's scalp trophies twisted and danced as the wind took them, and an aura of death abounded. Smoke from the burning corpses caught Isaiah's nostrils as he glanced back south.

He heaved the bodies of his wife and son onto the platform next to Rimmer's remains, and in accordance with Watseka's beliefs he led her pony into the sacred circle, and with one shot from the Collier, ended its life. His spirit would carry her and Little Dark on their final journey.

He then stood back and whispered a last farewell.

The hawk fluttered high beneath the scudding

clouds, diving and rising in the wind. Isaiah watched it descend, and then it would rise again, only to drop suddenly, then glide smoothly into ever decreasing circles until it landed on the body of Watseka.

As the wind ruffled its feathers it lifted its head and eyed Isaiah. Then with a screech like a voice from a netherworld it flew back skyward until it became a tiny speck and the pull of ethereal force gave way to absence and desolation and the significance of Watseka's dreams then gave up their meaning.

Back where she had always been, by Rimmer's side, she was with him once again; the thought struck Isaiah as he rode back to where the murderers' ponies were tethered. Perhaps his union with Watseka was never destined for longevity and that Rimmer would always regain her, even in death, and that he, Isaiah, was merely the custodian of her until she and Rimmer became reunited for the final time.

Smoke and flames roaring through gaps in the trees from the burning bodies and scorched coral posts had caused the tethered ponies to become skittish, and they bolted down in the direction of the valley bottom when Isaiah cut them loose.

18

The tracks of Wanoka's abductors ran down a steepish rocky and scrub incline that led to the northern end of the valley and by early afternoon Isaiah had reached the valley bottom. Rain clouds had now blown in with the keen wind and sharp spits flecked the dry ground.

As he rode through woodland the rain became heavier and its beat roared on the dense foliage above. The tracks through the leaf-mould-packed ground were clear and the occasional pony dropping betrayed the abductors' advance even more.

On he rode as the drenching wind hissed and whispered through swaying branches, and with the rain, stinging forest debris whipped up and formed aerial eddies. In the gloom the towering trunks appeared like sentinels stretching for miles under a light-killing canopy.

At one point the tracks became faint. Isaiah dismounted and studied the ground, then some distance further on, once again, they appeared deeper, more pronounced.

He reached a glade in which the abductors appeared to have rested. More pony shit lay under overhanging branches and once more a scattering of tiny coloured beads glinting on the leaf-mould-packed ground gave boost to his flagging spirits.

He rode on until dusk fell.

The forest became more sparse, thinning out into intermittent glades, then the track widened into rocky terrain, leading to the great northern pass with its dark peaks looming high.

He rode into the mouth of the pass as the silhouetted fringes of pines on the high bluffs against dying streaks of turquoise-blue light began to fade with the fall of night.

He rode on into the blackness as the rain became finer and the driving wind abated. Intermittent streaks of moonlight shone through occasional cloud breaks illuminating the dark forest outcrops so that they appeared to move like ghosts in a dreamworld.

Racked with the draining fatigue of trauma and with his buffalo robe and breaches sodden, he scanned the gloom for a rock niche where he could take respite for a few hours. After some distance and through the moonlight he reached a sheltered gully overhung with branches. Here he tethered his pony and pack mule, took a drink from his water sack and a pull of pemmican.

Dry tinder was impossible to find, so he lay back against the rock wall and shivered in the damp mist of the night.

Sleep would take him intermittently and he would wake through pulses of anxiety, heart pounding with the fatty pemmican surging in his gullet.

By first light he rode on and by mid-morning the rain had cleared, however the keen wind had again whipped up and remained unabated.

The pass widened at its northern end and the track broke out into mist-laden meadows fringed by grey elder. In the haze the dark form of a moose fed on leaves hanging from low branches.

As he rode the meadow Isaiah became aware of a low humming, and by dint of its softness it seemed to carry clear on the wind. A distant mounted figure came into view. As the figure approached it became clear that it was a mountain man, humming as he rode. He was mounted on a mule with two pack mules in tow, laden with skins. Occasional puffs of smoke were instantly whipped away by the wind.

Both men came to a halt.

The man appeared to be a seasoned trapper. He was heavily bearded and on his head was a curious tallowed hide bonnet tied under his chin with rawhide. Two feathers hung down from the rawhide thongs. He wore a belted buffalo robe, fur inwards, and buckskin leggings with twelve inch fringes. From his lips hung a great drooping pipe with a huge bone tobacco bowl, and intermittent clouds of smoke obliterated his face. A fine Hawken rifle with polished stocks and brass plates hung from a harness on his mule and round his neck hung a bone powder horn.

"Whar ye headed, son?"

"North, tracking men who murdered my wife and son and abducted my daughter."

"Red coons?"

"No, white."

"Whal from what ah seen back thar looks like ye headed right."

The man spoke with a rambling frontier brogue, typical of his breed and never paused.

"Remnints of a cold camp back thar, mebe ten mile, give a take one. Indin ponies two of 'em; no mules. Tracks headin' roughly ide say norwest. One set a har's breath deepern t'other. Indicates ter me a double rider, mebe a chile. Looks like ye headin' right. Only other thing ah took note of, cut the tracks of what ah took ter be a huntin' party. Assiniboin ah deduce headin' ah reckon west, no need ter watch ye hare, thar friendly. Bloods farther north, more'an likely lose ye top knot up thar."

He paused and took another draw on his enormous pipe. He then dug deep into one of his saddlebags and pulled out something wrapped in a large rolled leaf and handed it to Isaiah.

"Pickled buffala tongue. Aint much game up ahead."

And with another huge cloud of tobacco smoke he nudged his mule and continued on his way, humming as he rode.

Isaiah rode on through the rain-fresh meadow. A startled sage grouse flew skyward and then away toward woodland.

The flat, high-grassed meadows finally gave way to high bluffs and more mountainous terrain leading to canyons.

Sure enough at the base of the bluffs, in a glade surrounded by copse, was evidence of a cold camp. Deep pools of rainwater lay in gullies at the edges of the meadow.

The ground had been trampled and chips of wind-dried pony shit lay amongst the two sets of tracks running north toward the canyon. Ash scrapings from a pipe bowl were scattered where the men had sat on the flattened grass, and discarded chewed bones also lay nearby. Isaiah's pony and mule drank from the rainwater pools and grazed for a short while on the tall grasses, then he rode on, following the tracks into the mouth of the canyon, eating up miles until dusk finally fell.

The grinding of the animals' hooves on the rocky

canyon bottom echoed through its passages. Again scudding clouds above occasionally revealed bursts of blue light.

Once again fatigue took him and as night fell he made camp in a shallow cave in the canyon wall. He made fire with the dry brush that grew in the back of the cave. He took a bite of the pickled buffalo tongue; it tasted sharp, pungent but tender. He washed it down with a pull from his water sack.

Futile thoughts of Watseka then began to haunt him and wrestle them from his mind he could not. Finally he lay back on his buffalo robe and deep sleep took him.

In a dream she came to him; he felt her writhing under him, sensed the whisper of her breath, her cool touch on his neck, became intoxicated by her fragrance. He struggled for sight of her through roaring, rhythmic, distant chanting, then the hawk tore with ripping talons the sense and spirit of her from an intangible drifting presence, and once again soared away high into an enigma of the subconscious. He woke suddenly, aimlessly groping toward the dying embers of his fire, then like a beast in torment he sobbed and emitted a cry that transmuted to a roar that echoed back through the canyon, before being lost to infinity, and a wolf howled in the black distance as if to answer.

Sleep would not come to him again that night so he decided to ride on. The sky had cleared and the canyon tracks had become lit by moonlight. By first light he emerged from the canyon's mouth and rode on down a woodland-lined rocky track that led to a valley veiled in mist, banked either side by densely forested pines. A small herd of buffalo grazed in the distance to the east.

The sky was dense with grey cloud and a fine drenching rain blew on a soft wind. The tracks through the valley were faint, however marked by the occasional pony dropping. At the end of the valley the wooded hills either side began to flatten and run into a vast grassy plain, and at the end of the plain, barely visible through the mist, rose another mountain range.

By a small brook Isaiah came across the ashes of a fire, more pony shit and trampled ground. He watered his animals at the brook, allowed them to graze on fresh sprouting greenery beneath the trees and then rode on.

Some miles on across the great plain riders came into view through the mist-laden distance. As they approached steel glinted in the grey light and flashes of colour danced with rhythmic canter. Loose and braided hair tossed as they came on. The rattle of charms and vision quest talismans drifted on the wind as they rode closer. Isaiah held his ground and rode toward them at a steady lope.

There were twelve warriors in all; impressive men of stoic countenance, muscular, with hide shields and otterskin quivers strapped to their backs. Some had scalp trophies hanging from their lances and bows with the blood barely congealed. Four ponies at their rear bore the bloodied corpses of dead comrades.

As they rode closer Isaiah recognised them as Crow. The lead warrior raised an arm and the war party came to a halt. The Crow leader's beak-shaped face was masked in white clay mixed with tallow. He wore a porcupine quill bonnet which framed his features and he resembled a night owl observing prey. A blood-streaked gash on the shoulder of his elkskin shirt betrayed evidence of a recent skirmish.

Isaiah was known to him, word of his prowess at the Sun Dance had travelled far.

He informed Isaiah that the men he sought were headed north toward the Beaverhead mountains and that they were no more than a day's ride ahead.

North, relentlessly north!

The gestures and ramblings of the old man of Yellowstone suddenly flashed through Isaiah's mind.

The Crow leader continued: "Our enemies have rubbed out four of our brothers and you ride into their land. In past moons you have killed them and they revere you; a strong spirit guides you and it is known that the path you ride will be clear."

He then raised an arm and with a cacophony of hoof beats and rattling weapons the war party rode on. Isaiah caught the odour of the blood of their dead as they passed and then watched them slowly diminish into the misty distance.

He rode on, following the grass-trampled tracks across the great plain, eating up the miles. The sky had cleared and with the wind great billowing cumulus banked the Beaverhead range and by dusk he entered the foothills.

He rested in a grove by a shallow stream. The animals drank and grazed on high grasses. He rode on. Moonlight created soft shadows amongst the rocks and woodland and the black night glittered with galaxies. The way would be clear, and he rode on through the night. Wanoka was close.

The following day dawned clear and brilliant, and Isaiah's spirits were somewhat raised by the warmth of the sun on his back.

He rode a high ridge following tracks that now veered north-west and by late afternoon a column of smoke was visible around a mile distant, rising from what appeared to be a ravine.

Just before dusk Isaiah tethered his animals in a copse and with the Collier primed and cocked and his knife and hatchet in his belt he proceeded on foot. He crept by stealth through dense woodland toward the column of drifting smoke to the edge of the ravine and peered down from its rim.

Roughly built against the back wall of the ravine was a rambling cabin. The woodsmoke drifted from a crude drystone chimney poking through a sod roof. Pale yellow light glowed from its crude windows. Two ponies were corralled to the right of the cabin.

A pipe-smoking figure with lank black hair and rifle across his knees sat on a log pile with his back to the cabin. With silent surefootedness Isaiah descended the rocky incline that led to the ravine bottom.

Life for the pipe-smoking man ended in a moment. The honed blade of Isaiah's Green River was in the man's neck within seconds, the clay pipe fell from his lips as he slumped forward, squirmed like a severed worm and then spasmed on the ground amid jetting blood.

Isaiah crept to the window of the cabin. A fire blazed in a great stone niche. With his back to the window and facing the fire was seated a huge figure dressed in soiled black linen. The glow of the fire illuminated his great head and mountainous shoulders.

Wanoka sat on a bench against the cabin wall. She was naked, pale, trembling and sobbing intermittently. Her arms were purple with bruising.

The wall above the great fire appeared to be a shrine dedicated to God's waning power. Icons signifying that the balance between Christ's struggle and the force of evil were being drawn in Lucifer's favour. Black, burned and deconstructed crucifixes hung in disarray and with them the Trishul smeared in blood on a piece of hide screamed its chilling message.

Simmering with fury Isaiah burst into the cabin.

Wanoka shrieked, crying "Papa, Papa" in Crow.

Peter Stiener slowly turned, then stood with his back to the fire, his great dark form shielding Wanoka. Stunned, Isaiah recoiled at the sight of him, and speechless he levelled the Collier.

His father moved slowly toward him; a lumbering figure still possessing the aura of old – penetrating and disarming.

Deranged from neurosyphilis, his face was bloated, florid and ulcerated. His hair had thinned from the disease and hung in strands to his shoulders. His lips were coated with a white scum and saliva bubbled from the corners of his mouth.

"He above that most serve is defeated," he moaned, and with a voice distorted by insanity he went on: "His credence dies with each passing black night, and I know of dark victory, of devoured souls; insatiable, insatiable hunger. No wait!" And raising his arms he roared, "It has been satisfied, but only for a moment, your savage wife has been taken and the spawn of the filth from your loins will follow."

And with a glare from his eyes born of increasing madness he raised his arms again and roared: "You, betrayal, betrayal!"

The voice then descended into spluttering gibberish. "Tear the flesh, tear the flesh, devour,

devour and give up, give up, raise up. The blood is mine. Cut deep, deep smear the seed of death. Take them! Take them!"

Then a wave of unreality began to distort Isaiah's sense of reason and for a brief moment he froze and relaxed his grip on the Collier, and with a backhanded swipe Peter Stiener hit the weapon from his hand. A second blow summoned from a force of a dark unknown knocked Isaiah to the floor. Wanoka screamed as urine trickled down her leg and pooled on the wooden bench.

Then like a felled oak Peter Stiener slammed down on his son, and with demented murmuring began raining down blows to his son's head.

Isaiah took the blows one after another and gripped by a strange reticence, at that moment, could not summon the will to defend himself.

Wanoka screamed again, leapt from her bench, picked up the Collier and pushed it into her father's groping hand.

The blows kept coming and as they came thoughts of Watseka's dying breath and the bloodied form of Little Dark reared in Isaiah's mind.

The bullet from the Collier ploughed up through Peter Stiener's intestines and exited through his spinal cord. The second blew away the base of his jaw and drilled upward through the right side of his brain, lodging in the abnormal thickness of his huge skull. His father's blood gushed onto

Isaiah's chest as he remained upright for a few seconds before keeling sideways. Isaiah then dragged himself from under his father's great weight.

Wanoka flew to him throwing her arms round his neck. He held her as she wept uncontrollably in choking sobs, her tears saturating his blood-spattered beard, and she would not leave him. He calmed her, wiped her tears and wrapped her in a blanket. He leant her against a tree outside the cabin and she cried for him, and he calmed her again and assured her that he would never leave her.

He decided to burn the cabin to erase the evil that it embodied and cremate his father.

He dragged the body of the pipe-smoking man into the cabin. His daughter's eyes never left him. He fished embers from the fire and scattered them against the log walls.

Outside he freed the two corralled ponies and gathered Wanoka in his arms, stood back and watched the fire take hold. Flames engulfed the interior of the cabin within minutes. Blue smoke billowed from its windows and writhed and twisted in columns before the breeze took it. The fire spat and screamed its vicious torment and the flames danced blue and green until the scorched rafters gave way and the sods on the roof fell and sparks and flames floated upward.

When night fell the cabin and Peter Stiener were

reduced to embers that glowed, shimmered and pulsed in the black ash.

A sudden sharp gust then howled through the ravine lifting the ash in clouds. Spots of rain fizzed into the embers and thunder rumbled to the west, and like an exorcism all was finished.

19

Isaiah carried his daughter back up the rocky incline to where his animals were tethered. He dressed her in the beaded doeskin frock and moccasins that her mother had fashioned and draped a robe round her shoulders. She did not speak, her eyes were wide and she trembled still as he lifted her onto his pony. He mounted and with her in front of him he began the journey toward civilisation where the sun would rise.

He rode back through the night, away from the country of the Bloods and the land of the Snakes.

His intention was to ride south-west until he hit the Oregon Trail and then on to Leavenworth and finally by riverboat back to St Louis.

Three hours before dawn he decided to rest in a deep cave toward the end of a rocky pass that broke out into meadows. White bones and scattered lumps of charcoal and ash on the floor of the cave indicated that it had been a place of rest for other travellers who had passed that way. On the wall of the cave, drawn in charcoal, was the image of a running antelope with arrows embedded in its hind quarters.

He made fire and sat Wanoka to warm herself. She drank deep from his water sack but had no stomach for pemmican. With the warmth of the fire and exhausted by trauma, sleep quickly took her.

They both slept until dawn broke. When she woke panic took her and she cried out breathless until she was calmed by the sight of him.

The time of the Pink Moon was drawing to a close and fresh shoots of renewal flecked the meadows, valleys and plains, however dense cloud continued to obliterate the sun and they rode on that morning through fine drenching rain.

By evening the rain had abated and they camped in a great hollow shrouded by woodland that fringed the meadows.

In spite of the damp Isaiah managed to make fire with dry leaves and twigs gathered from the back of the hollow, and once again Wanoka would not eat but drank deep of water. She appeared pale and thinner, and devoid of her usual innate vigour and vivaciousness, and by dawn a mild fever had taken her.

The seasons were with them with the coming of

summer and therefore they were rich in time, and he decided not to ride on but rest up that day.

He kept the fire alive and with sleep and water she grew brighter. He made tea from yarrow leaves that grew nearby. She sipped the tea and drowsiness took her once again.

The land was silent save for a subtle sigh of a breeze in the whispering foliage. His animals grazed while he sat with her and the rest became a brief time of reflection, and he made harrowing entries in his journal.

So far Wanoka had not spoken of the murder of her brother nor the beating of her mother and Isaiah deduced that she must have been taken before these brutal events had occurred. Question their whereabouts she inevitably would and he agonised on how he would explain the fact that she would never have sight of them again.

Whilst gazing across the meadow he spotted movement a short distance away. A sage grouse pecked and foraged its way through high grasses. He went for the handle of his hatchet, raised it and hurled it at the grouse. Sensing air movement the grouse took off, however a fraction late; the hatchet clipped its wing and the bird floundered and fluttered to the ground.

Isaiah was on it in seconds and quickly rang its neck.

He roasted the bird on a spit and its fat sizzled in the embers and its rich odour permeated the hollow.

He devoured the bird that evening and tried to tempt Wanoka with small pieces of breast meat. He made her more yarrow tea and by dawn her temperature had almost returned to normal and so that morning they resumed their journey.

They rode on day after day through valleys, mountain tracks and across plains, all the while toward the light that heralded dawn. Each day Wanoka grew stronger and her appetite returned, though not for meat; she sustained herself on a diet of chicken berries and purple-black salal which grew in abundance.

By early June, the Strawberry Moon, the skies of billowing cloud had given way to days of crystal blue and high heat. Wanoka shed her robe and wore only her doeskin frock and a sun bonnet.

The occasional crooked tree marker planted by the old ones denoted a trail that had been ridden through time. Sometimes where the trail was cut or widened there were small rock piles that had been carefully assembled, and in some woodland glades there were remnants of campfire ashes, scattered bones and flesh reduced to carrion, with trampled pony tracks that led off through the trees.

It was evening when they rode through the foothills of the South Pass.

Horsemen appeared on a rise, black and deep

violet against the setting sun. Lances spiked the horizon as the ponies pranced and mingled. Loose hair, feathers and horns tossed in the fading light, and barking voices drifted on the evening breeze. They rode parallel on the crest of the rise for a mile and then with a cry and raised lance they disappeared down into the midge-infested western haze.

Some miles into the South Pass two riders came into view from round a bend in the rocky track. As they drew closer it became clear that the lead rider was a trapper. He rode a mule and under a wide-brimmed hide hat the man's bearded face was weathered dark. He was dressed in animal skins and wore a wolf-claw necklace. A wide-bladed skinning knife hung sheathed on his right hip. A powder horn and pouch were cross-strapped on his chest, and what appeared to be a well-worn, long-barrelled sixty caliber rifle rested across the horn of his apishamore. Behind him rode an Indian woman with a baby strapped to her back in a cradle board. In tow behind the woman was a pack mule laden with hides.

The two men came to a halt and nodded in recognition. Facial hair completely masked the man's upper lip.

"Torblence 'a brewin' ter the north," he said glancing back. His voice rang with the old familiar intonation of Rimmer's breed.

Isaiah scanned the northern hills and mountainous yellow-grey clouds were banking southward and a sharp breeze suddenly whipped up bringing with it a damp freshness to the air, and thunder echoed across the distance.

The man perused Isaiah for some time.

"Thar's somethin' farmilyer 'bout ye, recollect ye were at Popo Agie some years back. Rimmer's boy, warn't ye?"

"That I was."

"Heeard he'd gone Beaver."

"Yep, old Josh is no more. Bug's Boys' war club finished him."

Isaiah then fished out his tobacco pouch and filled his pipe bowl in readiness for a smoke at his next camp. After, he offered the pouch to the man who also stuffed the moist shag into the bowl of his pipe.

"Ah thankee," he said.

Both men then sat their mounts in silence for a short while.

The man then continued: "Fur trade's gone under, aint no Rendezvous no more. Got no more'an the price of a mule's prick this year gone for damn fine pews. Ye headin' fer th'Oregon trail?"

"Yep, Leavenworth, then St Louis; taking my daughter back to Virginia," replied Isaiah.

"Aint cast a bead on no town nor city for nigh on twenty year. Been holed up wit the Arikara, married one of 'em," the man said, rocking his head back in the direction of his stony-faced wife.

She was narrow-eyed and flat-faced, however her thick hair glinted in the early evening light. She wore a fringed doeskin robe, in places dark with grease, and over her shoulders hung a heavy hide cape. Cheap coloured bangles covered her arms and wrists.

"Heerd up north the Blackfeet and Snakes been hit hard be smallpox. Now thar's a thing; took a white man's pox ter defeat them infernal devils. Wish ye well, son."

And with that he urged his mule and he and his woman rode on.

Isaiah turned and as he watched them ride away memories of Rimmer and of Rendezvous past drifted through his mind. The man was of a dying breed and he knew he would never see his like again.

As Isaiah and Wanoka rode on through the pass, storm clouds obliterated the sun and darkness crept over the hills. Ephemeral streaks of yellow light occasionally cut the darkness. Lightning like a razor slash stabbed the horizon and huge droplets began to pelt the land. They rode to a scrub-covered overhang and huddled for shelter. The blinding light struck the land again and a cannon shot of thunder reverberated through the pass. The rain then sheeted in tumultuous bursts so that rivulets ran through the pass's rocky path.

After the storm had passed the sky gradually cleared and sunlight slowly washed the land.

They rode on and finally cleared the pass which broke out into a high-grassed plain, and there, in the blue haze of the distance, the Oregon Trail came into view.

And as Isaiah spurred his pony it shuddered and came to a stumbling halt. Its front legs slowly splayed and it went down. Its back legs followed and it rolled onto its side. Isaiah sprang clear. Its rump and ribs were lathered, its eyes rolled and foam oozed from its bit. Isaiah stroked its head and neck, and with a guttural grunt and a putrid hiss from deep in its throat it breathed its last.

Wanoka looked on perched on the mule as Isaiah cut steaks from the pony's rump and hung them on the mule's rear. Then they rode on.

Mounted on the indefatigable mule, who showed no signs of flagging, they cut the Oregon Trail around late afternoon. Their progress took them almost parallel to the Platte River, a line of light in the fading sun. They camped that night amongst the cottonwood groves that ran east along the line of the Platte and Isaiah roasted the rump meat of his dead pony, and as the stringy meat sizzled and smoked he paid silent homage to the animal that had bore him for mile after tortuous mile, and even in death continued to sustain him.

They continued east along the Oregon Trail that cut through undulating, rolling plains towards Independence, and as dusk began to fall on the second day, smoke columns became visible in the distance. Tiny flecks of yellow light illuminated dark forms around half a mile north of the trail.

The train of prairie schooners was large, around twenty five wagons drawn into a huge circle. Woodsmoke and the fatty odour of bubbling stew pots hung in the still air under a vast star-flecked night sky. Gaunt and weary-looking men smoked and talked in groups. Women in bonnets and soiled, ground-trailing frocks bustled to and fro, and ragged, grubby-faced children laughed and shrieked. A large herd of oxen and horses grazed to the north of the wagons.

"Hello the camp," Isaiah called in mountain parlance, as he and Wanoka approached.

A youth wearing a felt hat, loose calico shirt and soiled dungarees strode toward them with an old model muzzle-loading rifle raised.

"Who comes here?" he called.

"I am a mountain man, sir, bound for Independence with my daughter. We would appreciate the shelter of your wagons for the night and the refill of our water sacks."

The soft light from the campfires touched

Isaiah's high cheek bones, his great fair beard and waist-length hair, and in the gloom loomed the spectre of a wild man, and after glancing at the young Indian form of Wanoka, the youth became suspicious.

"I do not think that I will let ye pass, sir. That girl looks Indin ter me and yer appearance looks as savage as some o' them wild heathens. Be on yer way, sir."

"Hold sway thar, boy." A woman's voice, thick and course, came from the darkness.

She was large and grey-haired. Her face was deeply lined and weather-darkened. A woollen shawl draped her shoulders and a leather apron was tied round her ample stomach. A short-stemmed bone and briar pipe hung from the corner of her mouth.

"That chile looks ter me like she's bin ailin', she aint nothin' but skin 'n bone. She's in need a sleep and feedin'. Bring her through, mister."

The youth with the rifle lowered it and stepped aside without a word, in total obeyance to the apparent matriarch.

Isaiah dismounted, lifted Wanoka from the mule and followed the woman to her wagon. The woman spread blankets on the ground around a fire. A cast iron pot of broth bubbled on an iron tripod over embers.

"We are about ter eat, sir. Sit yeself down with yer daughter."

The youth with the rifle crouched opposite Isaiah and eyeballed him. He was joined by two older men and a woman.

"These are ma three sons and ma daughter-in-law."

They all nodded with a serious countenance.

"We are Missourians. We aim ter claim land in Oregon and start farmin' as far and away from that cold Missouri rain as possible. What is yer name, sir?"

"My name is Stiener and my daughter is called Wanoka."

The woman said grace and then ladled the stew into tin bowls, handed a bowl to each person and placed a pile of half-burnt, misshapen biscuits in the centre by the fire.

The men dived forward, grabbed the biscuits, broke them up, and mixed them into the broth, and then commenced to shovel the mixture into their mouths.

Likewise Isaiah, not having eaten for a day and a half, downed his like a man possessed.

The salty stew contained chunks of cured pork and was thick with pearl barley. Wanoka found it palatable, eating only small amounts of the broth.

No words were exchanged as they all ate.

After Wanoka had eaten all she could, she fell asleep exhausted with her head on her father's lap.

The youth, the younger woman and one of his older brothers left the fire after they had cleared their plates and returned to their wagons. The third brother remained and leant back against the wheel of the wagon.

The matriarch tossed the tin plates into a bucket of water and course soda and then sat down on an upturned wooden crate in front of the fading fire and lit her pipe.

"What happened ter that chile's mother?" she said, blowing out smoke and fixing Isaiah with a formidable stare.

"Her mother was a Crow Indian. She was murdered in the mountains; my small son was murdered with her."

"Dear Lord, sir. Were they killed by red devils?"

"No, my wife was beaten and raped to death by white men and before they raped her they butchered my son. Be wary of the land you are entering, ma'am. It can be brutal and unforgiving."

Isaiah then filled the bowl of his own pipe, lit it with an ember, drew deep and blew the smoke into the dying fire.

A silence then ensued whilst Isaiah gathered his thoughts, and the woman's gaze never left him.

"Her mother meant more to me than life itself. She laid bare my inner being, she touched my soul and I wanted her for every moment of the day, and I am to this day ripped apart with grief that she was taken from me. I know I will never meet her like again. She was called Watseka and I can be thankful that whenever I cast eyes on my daughter she lives on in my memory. I dedicate my life to her now, and I will do everything in my power to keep her safe."

"What happened to yer wife's killers?"

Isaiah allowed the pipesmoke to drift upward and stared into the fire.

"I killed them. Two other men made off with Wanoka; I tracked them down and killed them. I have had my vengeance, however I am left bereft."

"Yer story shocks me, sir. Ye have ma sympathy," said the matriarch, drawing deep on her pipe.

"I too am sorry for yer loss, sir," said the youth's older brother.

Then he and Isaiah stared into the fire in silence for some time.

A wailing, less than tuneful violin, struck up from one of the distant wagons and oxen bellowed in the night.

"Yer daughter can sleep with me in ma wagon. She will be safe. You, sir, can sleep under it. The train leaves at dawn. As you are headin' east, sir, I would be minded to dress that chile with consideration ter her wellbein'. She needs clothin' more appropriate than them animal skins."

Despite the woman's good intentions Isaiah's response was tainted with a flash of annoyance.

"Her mother fashioned that robe, and those animal skins as you call them have served her well over many, many miles."

"I appreciate that, sir, and that's as it mabe, but ah stand by ma words."

Isaiah lifted the sleeping Wanoka into the woman's wagon and covered her with blankets. He then returned to the fire and continued to smoke.

The matriarch disappeared for a short while and then returned with a neat pile of clothes. There was cotton underwear, woollen dresses, knitted stockings, a woollen coat and leather boots.

"Mr Stiener, I want ye ter have these. They belonged ter ma granddaughter. It grieves me ter tell you that she passed away on the trail, not two weeks gone. She was the same age as yer daughter and the same slight of build. She came down with a fever; her upper body was covered with a rash and it hurt her eyes ter look at the light. All I could do was sponge her down; she burned up for days. I could do nothin' else ter save her, and after a real bad night we lost her at dawn. We buried her in a cottonwood grove some miles back."

Isaiah exhaled with a deep smoke-filled sigh, and was momentarily taken aback by the gesture and the cloud of remorse in the matriarch's eyes.

"Ma'am, words fail me and I am humbled," he said. "I have money. Allow me to pay for them."

"No, sir. If these garments keep yer daughter warm and comfortable, that's payment enough for me."

The long night passed through the low murmur of the sleeping train, and sometime before sunrise the camp slowly erupted into general bustle and hubbub. Raised voices broke the silence, mules brayed, oxen grunted as they were led to be hitched to wagon shafts. The smoke from revived campfires mingled with the odour of bubbling coffee pots and frying bacon.

The matriarch handed Isaiah a tin mug of coffee and coaxed the blurry-eyed Wanoka into sipping a bowl of ox milk. Streaks of yellow light gradually slashed the horizon as the sun rose to burn off a low mist that hung over the prairie, and finally in the brilliance of a sultry dawn, the great train of wagons moved off onto the dust-grinding trail, and after giving thanks to the matriarch, Isaiah and his daughter rode on toward the east.

20

Dashes of light struck the walls of Fort Leavenworth in the heat of the afternoon as Isaiah and Wanoka loped in on a mule that was virtually spent. The fort sat on bluffs overlooking the Missouri. Isaiah dismounted and led his exhausted mount into a tranquil grassy square surrounded by barracks and officers' quarters in the centre of the fort.

Isaiah presented a towering, hide-clad presence in the quartermaster's stores with a heavy coating of trail dust covering his beard, shoulders and hide hat. Wanoka stood beside him, dwarfed by his size, her hair touched by the sun and with a subtle bloom in her complexion. She was given sticks of barley sugar, and outside the mule drank from a trough and grazed on the sweet grass of the square.

Isaiah purchased a quantity of army hard tack

and dried fruit as supplies for the twenty-day river voyage ahead.

Fortune had favoured them with the timing of their arrival. The riverboat Escandale lay at its mooring and was due to depart the following morning.

A motley gathering of characters, trappers, hunters, half-breeds, and traders, together with livestock, lounged, gambled, smoked and harangued on the riverbank and in the shade of cottonwoods, all waiting to board the Escandale at first light.

The following morning, after hours of general confusion, noise and hubbub, with a low blast on her whistle, amid shouts, cheers and gunshots, the river steamer cast off and shuddered and surged out into the Missouri and headed east down river.

Isaiah stood in the stern with Wanoka and gazed back west through gaps in the cottonwoods to the violet haze of serene peaks and drew deep on the stem of his pipe and exhaled. And with the fragrance of tobacco smoke endeavoured to exorcise a yearning that would not die. He struggled to stifle the recall of rhythmic distant chants born of a sacred circle and of a wind that never ceased, of the memory of woodsmoke-tainted air at twilight and the fatty juices of a fresh roasted kill, of fast-running streams rich in beaver, and Rimmer's rasping voice cursing in the killing frost of a winter mountain morning. And most of all of the husky sigh of the woman who had obsessed him and of whom he had loved.

Through sun-baked days under endless cloudless skies the riverboat toiled the Missouri currents, sometimes floundering on sandbanks; on and on she steamed through vast plains and treeless prairies dotted with black bison.

On the packed decks men whiled away the hours smoking, gambling and occasionally taking potshots at low-flying birds or a foraging elk that had strayed close to the shore.

One evening gunshots were heard from the lower deck. A whisky-fuelled altercation flared up between a trader and a mountain man and pistols were raised. The trader missed, the mountain man did not, and the trader took a ball through the heart killing him instantly. The dispute was unanimously declared a fair fight and the trader's body was unconventionally heaved over into the river. Isaiah did his best to shield Wanoka from the spectacle.

This was the only occasion that blood was spilled and the voyage from there on remained uneventful.

The Escandale steamed on relentlessly, and south-easterly breezes occasionally moderated the heat. There were times when Wanoka became beset by boredom, restlessness and irritability. She sipped water constantly, however her desire for food waned once again and her frailty gave concern. And there were times when Isaiah would hum to her in rich low tones and she would respond and pick up the melody in uncannily fine pitch. And there were also times when her restlessness could not be calmed and tearful tantrums would run their course.

The Escandale made remarkably good time, assisted by fast, down river currents and on the morning of the eighteenth day buildings and wharves were just visible through tree-lined shores in the hazy distance, and gunshots and cheers were raised on the first sighting of St Louis.

She pulled on through the great confluence waters of the Missouri and the Mississippi and finally into the wharves of St Louis. Steamboats lay moored in the muddy waters and the jetties bustled with life. In a decade St Louis, from its beginning as a small busy town, had now erupted into a teaming city.

With Wanoka, Isaiah disembarked with the chaotic rabble of tired, restless men and animals and rode away on the mule through the dusty packed-dirt streets in the direction of Ernest's general store. Neighbourhoods had sprawled, new taverns had sprung up, and there were stables, forges and street traders where before there had been scrubland.

Ernest's store was unchanged save the name above the door; it read *Guttman and Sons, Merchandise*. Mystified, Isaiah dismounted, tethered the mule and entered the store. A concoction of odours, of leather, iron, methylated spirit and ground coffee sent a nostalgic jolt to his memory.

The layout of the store was different and the outhouse at the back had been extended. The doorway was lit by daylight from a rear window and the memory of Miguela's frail form framed by the light flashed into his mind.

A pale, balding, gawky man in a leather apron stood behind a rough-sawn, planked counter. A similarly built young man glanced back as he stacked and re-arranged shelves at the rear.

"Afternoon, sir. I'm looking for Ernest Hackett. He used to be the proprietor here."

The gaunt, slender man stared vacantly at Isaiah for some time before answering in a shaky voice that was at the same time deep and gravelly.

"By all accounts he died. I acquired this business from his wife some years back."

"And his wife, what happened to her?"

"I believe she still lives in a large house some miles west in open country."

Then pondering the man's words Isaiah scanned the store for a brief moment and finally drew out two sticks of barley sugar from a stoneware jar and handed the man what loose coin he had.

"I wish you well, sir," he said and then turned and strode out, mounted his mule on which Wanoka was perched and headed west out of the city.

. . .

Two women sat on the veranda of the pale weatherboarded house in the twilight. One was silver-haired and ageing, the other a negress of middle years.

Yellow flickering candlelight shone dimly through the slightly threadbare curtain lace of the windows. The house was in a state of disrepair. Thick moss grew on the roof tiles and the once brilliant white weatherboarding was blistered and flaking.

"Morena, Morena," the voice drifted.

Both women rose from their chairs and squinted into the fading light as he came on on the loping mule. He dismounted and lifted the tired and weak Wanoka down. He strode onto the veranda; his teeth flashed through the forest of his beard as he smiled at her and clutched her to him. He left her breathless with his embrace and her head spun from the power of him and she smelled the pungency of his deerskins, and sensed the pulse of his energy.

"I knew you would return," she said, trembling at his presence. "Dear God, I cannot believe it is you, but who is this child?"

Morena's expression then changed; it became enigmatic, a mix of intrigue and mild distain.

"She is my daughter."

Then in silence she studied Wanoka for some time before the negro woman ushered them all into a large front parlour.

Low candlelight glinted on the polished floorboards. The room smelled of beeswax in turpentine cut through by the occasional waft of simmering meat from the adjacent kitchen. Dried flowers in chipped earthenware vases stood on polished oak furniture. A worn leather sofa and two wicker armchairs with scattered cushions were arranged in front of a huge stone fireplace. A fading water colour of a sunset over the Sangre de Cristo Mountains hung above the thick oak mantle.

They all sat for a short while in silence as Morena studied Wanoka and tried to take in Isaiah's massive presence.

"This is Libby," she then said. "She lives with me. She is my companion and helper. And Libby, this is my nephew Isaiah. He has returned to us from the mountains."

Wanoka curled up on one of the wicker chairs and sleep quickly took her.

"By her appearance I would say that that child's mother was a squaw. Where is she now?"

Before answering Isaiah casually dug into his tobacco pouch and filled the bowl of his pipe, ramming the shag down with his thumb and lighting it with a taper Libby had fetched from the kitchen range.

"Dead! Together with my son."

"Dead! Dead how? And you also had a boy with the squaw?"

Isaiah then drew deep and exhaled the smoke.

"The tale is long and difficult, and there is not a day when the horror of what happened does not rear like a demon in my thoughts, and I am weary with the constant battle of its recall; and I do not wish to go into it now."

"Well, Isaiah, I am shocked by what you have told me, and this news is all too sudden. It is clear that you have had union with a woman of heathen beliefs; granted she is a beautiful child, nevertheless I am minded to tell you that I do not hold with any union outside the sanctity of a Christian marriage."

Morena then paused and began to finger the gold crucifix on her chest.

Another cloud of pipesmoke drifted through the flickering candles.

"Aunt, you are entitled to your beliefs, however I will not apologise for the love I felt for my Crow wife. We were married according to Crow ceremony. To me she was like no other woman.

"I left home because of the preposterous tyranny exerted by my father and I will not be bound by doctrines that have no basis in proof or evidence.

"The peoples west of the Missouri believe in the so-called Great Spirit that is supposed to permeate all life; I doubt that I subscribe to this notion either, however it has just as much credence as any other belief in the divine, and no Christian has the right to shout it down."

Libby continued to sit in silence, and Morena's eyes began to cloud with annoyance.

"I have stated my disapproval and I will not change my opinion. What you have done contradicts my Catholic beliefs, however I am not a callous woman, and I realise that you and that child have endured a long and dangerous journey, and you are both exhausted. Libby will give you food, and then you can both sleep in the back room."

Feeling uncomfortable and also mildly irritated Isaiah leant back into the sofa and removed the pipe from his lips.

"Miguela! Where is she and what of Uncle Ernest?"

"I am saddened to have to tell you that Miguela passed away some two years gone. She was taken by pneumonia. The infection went deep into her lungs; she was not strong enough to survive it, and we lost her in the space of just a few hours. As you know she meant everything to Ernest and he never came to terms with her passing and almost a year later he suffered an apoplectic seizure which has rendered him paralysed down his right side. He is a shadow of the man he was; he cannot walk or speak and he sleeps most of the time. I would be grateful if you spent a little time with him before you resume your journey."

Isaiah's tetchiness began to mellow with the revelation of her words.

"Of course, it goes without saying that I will," he replied.

The atmosphere the following morning at breakfast was mildly uncomfortable with Morena unrelenting in her attitude of disapproval, and her regard for Wanoka was less than gracious.

Isaiah made it clear that he intended to continue his journey east with Wanoka by coach within the next few days after he had disposed of his virtually broken mule.

Later that morning Morena showed him to Miguela's old room in which Ernest now slept.

Ernest sat upright in his bed propped against pillows. The room was rank with the musk of sickness and decline. Libby threw open the windows to freshen the air.

To Isaiah, Ernest was unrecognisable from the uncle he had known. His beard and what hair remained had turned pure white. His strong, broad, stocky frame had become emaciated and frail. His once powerful hands had become delicate, wrinkled and dotted with dark age stains. His right eye was almost closed and saliva trickled from the side of his drooping, twisted lips.

Icons of his adored daughter adorned the room. Her red Spanish dress hung from the teak wardrobe door. Her black boots, one with a built-up sole to compensate for her disability were positioned beneath the dress. Her gold earrings, her rosary and a lock of her black hair lay in a silver tray on the cabinet by his bed. Two portraits of her in black chalk hung on an adjacent wall and despite being toughened by his wilderness years Isaiah struggled to hold back his emotions.

"He will not let her go, he cannot bring himself to say goodbye," Morena whispered.

Then she leant close to him. "There is someone here to see you, Ernest. It is Isaiah, he has returned from the mountains."

Ernest stared with his one good eye. The black dye of its pupil dilated wide and apprehension appeared to cloud his features. An inaudible mumble then spluttered from the left side of his mouth. Morena wiped the saliva that dribbled into his beard.

"Ernest, please nod if you recognise him."

Isaiah lifted and stroked Ernest's left hand and as he did so a tear trickled into his moustache and his lips parted in his struggle to make an utterance. The left side of his mouth then raised slightly in a faint smile and he nodded.

"I will leave you with him. I would appreciate it if you sat with him for a while."

Morena and Libby then left the room.

That evening after dinner Morena's mood appeared to mellow. She became more amenable and conversation flowed, and in response to her occasional probing Isaiah began reluctantly to slowly unravel the story of his association with Rimmer and the events leading to Watseka's murder. However, the facts surrounding the killing of his father he kept close to his chest; they would go with him to the grave.

Morena listened in stunned silence. Then there was a long pause while she briefly composed herself and interjected: "Isaiah, as you speak, I have just remembered. I have something for you."

She left the room then returned with a letter and handed it to him.

"This was delivered for you some weeks after you left for the mountains."

Isaiah stared at the wax-sealed cream parchment. The quilled handwriting in blue ink was unmistakably his sister Bethel's.

"I will open it and read it later," he said, placing it upright on the mantle.

"Ernest wanted to read it; Miguela and I dissuaded him from opening it. We both considered that we had no right to open mail addressed to you."

"I appreciate that, Aunt," he replied.

After breakfast on the morning he was to leave Morena showed Isaiah to Ernest's huge mahogany wardrobe.

"Before you leave, if you wish, you may take your pick from Ernest's old clothes. He will never wear them again and there are some here he has never worn. He was always as broad as you. You may find his woollen jacket and boots will fit you and these shirts are of good quality heavy flax linen."

The farewell to Morena was not without slight misgivings, however Isaiah kissed her cheek and thanked her. She and Libby then watched him and Wanoka ride away into the distance, back toward the city.

21

Pulled by a team of four the coach trundled its way out of the city past weatherboarded houses and wooden shacks onto the churning dust of the main coach road east.

Breezes from the north-east had brought oppressive skies to replace summer heat, and gathering speed, the coach rocked and swayed into more open country past smallholdings, settlements and onward toward distant forested hills.

Opposite Isaiah sat two women dressed in black and an overweight balding man in a faded brown frock coat, snuff-stained at the lapels, smelling faintly of cigars and stale sweat.

The man caught Isaiah checking out the polished walnut butt of a pistol just visible at his ample waist inside his coat.

"Precaution, can't be too careful. Heard talk of

Kentucky road agents," he said, at the same time tapping the bulge in his coat with his fingers.

Dressed in Ernest's woollen jacket and linen shirt, Isaiah likewise sensed the assurance of the loaded Collier concealed in his deep inner breast pockets and nodded in agreement.

Next to Isaiah sat another man, younger, clean-shaven, reasonably well-dressed with a leather satchel on his lap and as the coach sped on he removed documents one by one from the satchel and studied them, occasionally mumbling a curse to himself whenever the coach jolted over ruts.

The two women spoke little, remained stony-faced, and glanced at Wanoka with an air of disdain whenever she became restless. Most of the time she occupied herself with two rag dolls that had once belonged to Miguela.

The fat man opposite Isaiah indulged in occasional small talk in an attempt to engage him in conversation; Isaiah's response, however, remained one of indifference in spite of the man's efforts.

Onward through the day the coach sped, and as dusk began to fall the sky cleared and a fading western light brightened the land as the coach pulled in at a rambling timber roadhouse.

Two pilgrims, an old man and a boy dressed in rags, sat outside on a wooden bench gnawing bones and drinking water from dented tin mugs.

Inside was a crude scrubbed pine bar and heavy

trestle tables on a rickety plank floor. Blue fumes from grilling meat drifted through from the scullery at the rear.

The coach teamsters sat themselves in the corner and were later served a platter of black grilled offal, cornbread and beer by a stern-faced woman in a filthy grey frock.

Isaiah ordered a bowl of stew and a pitcher of water. The stew was a steaming watery broth of turnips, potatoes, chunks of tough grey beef and gristle. Wanoka munched on an apple and drank the water.

As night fell the travellers were shown to two musty dormitories, one for men and one for women, each with rows of palliasses on wooden frames.

The two black-garbed women turned their noses up at the grubby beds, preferring to spend the night seated in the bar area.

After downing his meal and a pitcher of beer the fat man took to his palliasse, smoked two cigars, broke wind, and then grunted and mumbled his way into a deep, snore-interrupted sleep. The younger man settled down at the far end of the dormitory and continued to study his papers by candlelight into the night.

Wanoka fell asleep quickly. Isaiah lit his pipe, smoked for a while, and then in the relative peace of the late hour he opened Bethel's letter. It had lain unopened in Morena's possession for years. It read as follows:

Dear Isaiah,

I hope this letter finds you safe. Ma did inform me that you had departed for St Louis and would be staying with the Hackets. I fear it bears news of the worst kind. A dread of this moment has been with me for years, the moment when Father would go too far in one of his fits of fury, and it is with deepest regret that I have to inform you that the moment has arrived.

Ma is dead, murdered by his hand. Clara was witness to his rage and the blow from his fist that killed her.

As a result of the shock, Clara is now of an extremely delicate state of mind, however she did convey to me a rather garbled account of what happened. She described how Father arrived home late from one of his wanderings to discover that you had left home without his knowledge or consent. He accused Ma of encouraging you to leave, then flew into a rage and struck her. She fell back and hit her head on the wooden mantle. He then fled, riding off into the night.

Clara fears that he may be losing his mind and that he is out to track you down. A county warrant has now been issued for his arrest.

Ma has now been laid to rest and our sadness at her burial was deepened by your absence.

The old house is now unoccupied and Clara now lives with us.

God be with you wherever life takes you.

Love as always, Bethel.

After reading the letter Isaiah leaned back against the timber-planked wall and puffed pipesmoke into the gloom of the dormitory, and as he did so the sense of loss that already lingered within him fell to a new morbid low.

"Death treads in your shadow." Born of Pagan intuition, the words cut though time like a scythe in his memory, and truth as determined by destiny chilled his blood.

He sat for some time in thought and allowed the glow in his pipe to die. He gazed at the sleeping Wanoka and realised the meaning in the gift she had become to him.

Shafts of searing sunlight through cracks in the plank walls, Wanoka tugging at his beard and the bustle and yells of the teamsters woke him with a start.

Just after first light the teamsters had hitched the horses to the coach and begun calling the travellers to board. They each downed a mug of coffee cloudy with grounds, paid their dues to the roadhouse keeper and climbed into the coach.

The morning sunrise was glorious, casting a crisp, brilliant veridian, violet light over distant hills and forests.

The horses, fresh and well-fed, snorted and

reared their heads, and the exhilarating tang of pure morning air became tainted with the rich odour of their steaming dung.

Then with a yell and a lash from the teamsters the coach jolted, reared forward, rocked and gathered speed once again through the Kentucky landscape.

22

> The cosmos is a circular force and forms of existence are round. Seasons repeat themselves in circular fashion, always returning to where they began. The great sky is curved, and the course of life is a circle.
>
> – Thoughts of a holy man.

It was mid-afternoon when the coach pulled into the forecourt of the Pleasure Ridge Inn. The march of years had seen the inn develop into an important stopover for travellers bound for Virginia.

Before Isaiah climbed down from the coach he

studied the inn's façade and pondered the enigma of life's course that had delivered him full circle, and his thoughts then turned to Rosheen and their short union years before.

The inn had been extended; to the left an annex had been built to accommodate the growing number of travellers, and to the right more stables had been added with a blacksmith's forge. The original building was now cloaked in glorious wisteria with *Pleasure Ridge Inn* high on the wall in black iron letters framed by the foliage.

A boy unhitched the team and led them, their coats lathered and steaming, to the stables.

The travellers entered the inn one by one. Isaiah held back so that he and Wanoka would be last. A man with heavy side whiskers and moustache registered each guest in, after which they were shown to their rooms. The man stared in perplexed fashion at the approach of the big man with the long hair tied back in a ponytail, the heavy beard and weather-worn countenance.

The interior of the inn had also undergone extensive refurbishment. Through a corridor to the left was a large wood-panelled dining area with polished tables and chairs of maple and hickory. On the walls were guilt-framed landscapes depicting western scenes with dramatic skies. Two stags' heads on oak mounts adorned the walls above a gaping smoke-blackened cavern of a stone fireplace.

Through a corridor to the right was a bar tended by a short man with pomade-flattened hair. The bar was full of drinkers and redolent with tobacco smoke, and it buzzed with the low murmur of conversation. At the far end of the bar was a raised stage with an upright piano. With its success and resultant revenue the inn had acquired a noticeable aura of grandeur.

Isaiah followed the desk clerk up a flight of stairs, and reaching the landing he turned and glanced down, and as he did so a woman of some elegance dressed in a pale blue cotton dress, heavily-bosomed, with a black embroidered choker, her ashe-blonde hair pinned high with hanging ringlets, emerged from the door that led to the kitchen and walked briskly and with some purpose into the bar.

The years had witnessed a transformation in Rosheen from the raw simple girl to a mature woman of some sophistication.

To Isaiah the immediate impression was startling and he pondered her impressive appearance as he made his way to his room.

Once in their room Wanoka succumbed to sleep once again. Isaiah relaxed and smoked his pipe and contemplated his imminent reunion with Rosheen.

It was early evening when they made their way down to the dining area. Many of the guests were already seated, and the bewhiskered desk clerk, now turned waiter, and florid of face, was serving plates of food. Rich smells drifted from the kitchen at the rear.

Isaiah entered the bar. Rosheen was polishing glasses and had her back to him. As he approached she glanced up and saw his reflection in the backing mirror.

"Rosheen," he said, his voice soft and barely audible amid the general cacophony of drinkers' conversations.

She turned and fixed him with her gaze, her face expressionless.

With maturity she had become handsome, her complexion had not lined and had remained pale and fine-grained, and her facial expression had acquired an authoritative air.

"Remember me?" he said.

Isaiah's appearance, his beard and sun-darkened face momentarily threw her. Then after a few seconds, recognition dawned on her and her eyes brightened.

"I always knew it would only be a matter of time," she said.

She continued to stare at him, her lips parted as if to say more, however no words came. She then walked round from the bar, took his arm and led him to a corner table. They sat and her eyes never left him.

"You have changed," he said. "You have become very fine."

"So have you," she replied. "You left here a boy and you have returned a man."

Her eyes diverted to Wanoka.

"My daughter," he said.

"Are you married?"

"I was, my wife was killed."

She leaned across the table and placed her hand on his. "Forgive me if I struggle for words, I cannot quite take a grip on immediate reality. Your presence here has shaken me more than you realise. How far have you come?"

"From the Beaverhead mountains, and I fear the long journey may have weakened her," he replied, glancing toward Wanoka.

"What are your intentions? Do you have immediate plans?"

"I intend to travel on to where I was born and reunite with my sister Bethel. I will look for work, I have her to think of." He nodded again toward Wanoka. "She will require schooling; the future is uncertain. I have lived free in a life taking wilderness for years, and getting used to society's restrictions once again will not be easy for me."

Rosheen enquired no more and rose from her chair.

"I have work to do," she said. "I will arrange food for you and your daughter. We must talk more later."

He watched her walk back into the bar and immediately engage with guests. He noted how much more self-assured she had become, a contrast to the mildly withdrawn girl he had known when they had first met.

It was late in the evening when the final drinkers dispersed and the diners had retired to their rooms. Rosheen and her staff continued working in preparation for the following day.

Isaiah and Wanoka slept well that night and in the morning joined the other travellers for an early breakfast before the coach was due to depart.

Rosheen broke off from serving her guests, sat with him and drank coffee with him, and he lit his first pipe of the day.

Then she fixed him with a purposeful, penetrating stare and said, "Stay here for a few days longer with your daughter. She needs more rest after the journey she has endured. Please stay as my guest. There will be other coaches bound for Virginia."

Isaiah drew on his pipe and mulled over Rosheen's offer. He glanced at Wanoka, her tiny pinched face and her exhausted slight frame. He too was travel weary and also rich in time, and it did not take him long to agree.

After he had breakfasted he and Wanoka returned to their room and slept on until midmorning and the coach departed without them.

That afternoon Isaiah sat and smoked in the sun in the garden at the rear of the inn, and gazed toward woodland to the east and contemplated the prospect of a return to Virginia with a daughter who was half Crow.

Rosheen brought out a tray of tea, a beverage he had not taken for years, and they talked while Wanoka played.

"You have achieved so much here," he said.

"Remember my father?" she replied. "He passed away seven years ago, almost to the day. He always intended this inn to pass to me on his death. Since then I have worked ceaselessly to create what you see today. After he died I had no one and I had little choice but to be resourceful and strong. Being a woman the task of managing this inn has been fraught with problems and over the years I have had to deal with unscrupulous and violent men; and there were times when I would descend into black despair and contemplate failure. I do, however, have determination and I made up my mind that I would allow nothing to defeat me."

There was a long pause as she stared down at the ground in reflective mood, then she said, "Tell me about your wife, how did you lose her?"

Isaiah gazed into the distance once again and drew deep on his pipe. She stared at him in expectation and there was a silence when he appeared to drift, and after a while he began to recount the events of the saga of past years, of his association with Rimmer, and his ultimate death, and of his Crow marriage to Watseka and her brutal end.

He spoke of Watseka as if she were responsible for the stirrings of his soul. He spoke of her subliminal energy that seemed to saturate his psyche and create surges in his emotions that drove him in his desire. He spoke of the ethereal pull of her in past dreams that tore him from reality, and as he spoke Rosheen was at times left bereft and torn of emotion. However, her spirits rose when he intimated that recently she was beginning to fade in his memory and he was slowly rationalising the concept that Watseka could never have been anything other than an ephemeral force in his life and that she always was, and would forever be Rimmer's woman.

During the early hours of the following morning Isaiah stirred to the sound of his door opening softly. Wanoka slept soundly.

Rosheen stood before him silhouetted against pale light from the window. Her hair hung loose to her shoulders. She slowly slipped off her cotton gown and lay against him. She caught her breath as he embraced her and ran his hands down over her back and buttocks.

The years had seen her become slender, however

her breasts remained full and hung heavy. She struggled to suppress her panting for fear of waking Wanoka as he entered her. He lay on her with slow tenderness. The years between their last union appeared to transcribe in his mind into a mere flick of a page. Time had become meaningless as he embraced her once again.

She had become skilled as a lover. Her vaginal muscles teased his hardness with rippling pulses and he groaned softly in his ecstasy.

He worked into her with a gentle slowness and her orgasm began to erupt in slow spasms, building to a climax that made her weep.

After their lovemaking they lay in silence for a short while, then she whispered, "Stay here with me, think twice about moving on. Help me run this inn. You said that you would look for work. There is enough work here for two men. We can raise your daughter together. I have substantial savings that will pay for her education. I have it on good authority that I am barren, I can never experience childbirth. Perhaps your little daughter could fill that void within me."

Then she pulled back from him and fixed him with a gaze in the dim light.

"Please think on what I have said. Despite there having been other men in my life, you have never been far from my thoughts during the years that have passed. It has always been you."

And with that she quietly left his bed, slipped on her gown and made her way back to her room.

After she left he lay awake in the silence that was broken only by the faint breathing of Wanoka.

He had been stirred by their lovemaking and thoughts of her touch had made him desire her more. He had been impressed by her forthrightness and touching sincerity, and she had offered him and Wanoka the very future he had returned east to seek.

A second Virginia-bound coach had pulled in the day before and once again travellers were breakfasting before continuing their journey. As usual Isaiah sat smoking at one of the tables. Rosheen appeared flushed with eagerness as she brought him a pot of coffee.

"Will you board her?" she said, nodding out toward the forecourt.

After a silence he blew out a cloud of pipesmoke and shook his head, and as a faint smile gradually broke across his features, he said: "We will stay. You have offered me all that I left the mountains for. How could I refuse?"

The bloom in her cheeks deepened even more and her eyes brightened as she stared at him, and he caught the drift of lavender water as she turned, her skirts billowing with a spring in her step that marked a new dawn.

. . .

As was his wont, Isaiah powered into the work at the Pleasure Ridge Inn with unceasing energy.

In addition to countless other tasks he tilled, planted and cultivated the half acre of land at the rear of the inn. He also reared pigs, kept chickens and a small herd of goats; and as a result, the inn's kitchen was always well-stocked with produce and fresh meat, and as a slaughterman he was skilled, a testament to his years as a trapper.

He observed closely the work of the blacksmith, and slowly acquired the rudiments of the trade, and when the ageing blacksmith retired through ill health, Isaiah took over the forge and ironwork then became his passion.

After one year Isaiah and Rosheen married. The reception was a great affair. It was held at the inn and was attended by all Isaiah's sisters and their husbands including nephews and nieces Isaiah had never previously met.

His sister Bethany and her husband arrived with Clara Meek, who over the years had become chronically arthritic and was virtually wheelchair-bound.

Bethany's reunion, in particular with Isaiah, was poignant and at times tearful.

Celebrations continued for two days with considerable quantities of food and drink consumed.

During quiet moments Bethany frequently

raised with Isaiah the subject of their fugitive father. She made it clear that their father remained a wanted felon whom she believed was still at large and although he had apparently vanished without trace, and that no information as to his whereabouts had surfaced for over a decade, she still harboured a lingering fear that someday she would witness his return.

And during times when she thought of him, his voice would resonate in her mind and she would sometimes sense his presence, and in response, with an expression that betrayed no emotion whatsoever, Isaiah offered her words of possible reassurance, intimating that after over ten years, their father had more than likely vanished for good.

23

As the years passed Wanoka proved difficult to raise and Rosheen's own relationship with her was without doubt a trying one.

Her later childhood years were beset with periods of emotional fluctuations which ranged from relative contentment to irrational tantrums. There were times when she felt a churning sense of unrest that her young brain could not rationalise; a fleeting feeling of unbelonging when the pull of distant forces would come to her through the mix of her blood and in dreams.

Amnesia from her early childhood trauma began to release its grip through time.

Staccato flashes of semi-distorted visions would occasionally come to her in waves, in night terrors and a strange quasi sub-reality; a mother's face of serene beauty staring down, searing fear, muffled harsh gravel voices, looming intruders silhouetted in a doorway against pale light, a toddler's cry, a scream enmeshed in a wail of death, blurring blood smears and flailing limbs, raven-grey hair wrenched from its roots, ripped from primal arms, brutal power, away, away to rhythm-pounding hoof beats.

Whenever Rosheen woke in the dead of night to her screams, she would run to her and attempt to calm her. She would apply cold sponges to her body in an effort to bring her to consciousness, clamp her arms to subdue her, all too often to no avail. The demon in her would always do its worst, and eventually exhausted and whimpering she would lay back and sleep would take her once again, and in the morning she would remember nothing.

Rosheen engaged a number of private tutors to educate Wanoka. Few lasted longer than a number of weeks. All found the girl at times unreceptive to learning and occasionally rebellious.

Music, however, seemed to absorb her and there were many times when she and Isaiah would sing together in fine harmony.

Since her father's death Rosheen had continued his tradition of music at the inn. Once a month local musicians would gather at the inn and play for an entire evening.

Some evenings Wanoka would sing solo with her father by her side with a sweet voice that pulled drinkers to the bar, and when she sang she appeared to shed her inhibitions and project a persona that was totally endearing. When her voice reached out she became more compelling with every note, pause and crescendo, and as time passed word of her voice began to spread far.

By her late teenage years Wanoka had developed into a young woman of striking appearance. She stood almost six feet tall in her stockinged feet, and her body had blossomed strong and voluptuous. Her hair was thick, glossy and Crow black, the light glints of her childhood years had vanished, and when she woke in the morning it framed her face dark and wild. Her eyes swept back like petals to her temples under thick black arched brows. Her skin was not dark but delicately grained like fine vellum, and when she rouged her lips one glance from her could be disarming.

When she went walking men and boys would turn their heads. And sometimes she would wear the hawk bone earrings that had belonged to her mother, and then the Crow blood in her would simmer wild and Pagan, and rumour amongst the local good Christian women of Virginia would abound.

As the years passed her night terrors began to subside and the traumas that haunted her as a child also began to fade. With maturity she became grounded and her confidence blossomed, and eventually her relationship with her stepmother evolved into one of trust and affection.

Recognising Wanoka's talent, Rosheen engaged a singing and music tutor to coach her. She responded well to his teaching and carried out her voice exercises and practised her scales with daily discipline.

In due course her tutor became of the opinion that Wanoka was without doubt supremely gifted and possessed rare voice qualities, and that she should seriously consider training as a professional soprano. However, he considered that there was a limit to what he could teach her, and that eventually she should apply for a scholarship to study full-time at an academy of music and arts in Boston.

And so in the spring of her twentieth year, and accompanied by her stepmother, Wanoka journeyed to the Boston academy to be auditioned, and of the fifteen hopefuls who performed that day, only six were selected for scholarships of which the somewhat stoic Wanoka was one.

She began her studies in Boston in the autumn semester, and boarding in academy rooms was her first experience of life away from home.

After the first month of the semester Wanoka wrote home in a state of general unhappiness. She stated that her music course was extremely demanding and that there were times when she struggled to achieve the high standards required.

She also complained of being homesick and lonely, and she had begun to wonder what it was about her that made it so difficult for her to form friendships. However, in spite of all this, she stated that she would soldier on and see the course through come what may.

Then a few weeks before Christmas of that year she wrote again saying that her homesickness had passed and that she had struck up a friendship with a young man whose name was Rollo, who was studying to become a tenor, and that she was feeling much more content.

Struck by her extraordinary looks, a number of Boston young men, some full of bravado, had tried their luck and propositioned Wanoka. She, however, was left cold by all their advances, and it was only the shy, mild-mannered Rollo who always made her laugh, who had captured her interest and her attention.

It was during Wanoka's final year at the academy that Rosheen's health began to fail. Her weight loss was slow and insidious. She became listless and her characteristic boundless energy became dogged by bouts of fatigue.

She developed a rasping cough that sometimes would not abate. A local doctor diagnosed pneumonia in one of her lungs as a result of being rundown and mildly anaemic. He prescribed a diet rich in iron, rest, plenty of liquids, and regular supplements of tincture of quinine.

After a period of rest and with medication Rosheen appeared to improve and rose from her bed. However, her weight loss continued, and after a few days her cough returned and she took to her bed once again.

Then one night she woke gripped by a seizure and began to cough up a mixture of sputum and blood. She was feverish and Isaiah attempted to cool her with cold towels. The seizure finally passed and eventually sleep took her.

In the days ahead her coughing fits continued, each time with blood-streaked mucous expelled, and she grew weaker.

Extremely concerned, Isaiah called the local doctor once again. After a further examination the doctor confessed that he could do little more for her, and he advised that she should seek the opinion of a specialist in respiratory diseases, and that he could refer Rosheen to just such a physician at the local infirmary.

And so the following week a pale and drawn Rosheen, accompanied by Isaiah, journeyed to the infirmary, and in a small consulting room the specialist examined her.

His diagnosis was that she was suffering from tuberculosis and that unfortunately there was little treatment available other than fresh air, rest and mild expectorants that a pharmacy could prepare.

While Rosheen was dressing up the specialist took Isaiah to one side and quietly told him that he considered Rosheen's prognosis all but hopeless, and that the disease was slowly devastating her lungs, and that she would have at most a few months.

When they returned to the inn she took to her bed once again, overcome with fatigue.

"You do not need to tell me what the doctor said, I know that I do not have long," Rosheen whispered as they lay together that evening. "I know that my body is failing and that the power I always felt within me is now fading. However, I am content; we have achieved so much together."

Her voice then dropped to a whisper.

"I have had my will drafted in favour of you and Wanoka; I leave the Pleasure Ridge in your safe hands."

Isaiah made an attempt to reply then hesitated, gathered his thoughts and concluded that words at that moment would be inappropriate. Instead he drew her close and stroked her hair.

After a few weeks she appeared to rally and her symptoms began to ease, only for them to return days later with avengeance, and she grew weaker still.

. . .

It was around three in the morning when Rosheen raised herself from her pillow and reached for Isaiah. He took her arm and she leaned back on his chest. Her breathing was erratic and she burned with fever. He stroked her hair and they both gazed through the wide open windows into the black night toward woodland to the east.

A speck of yellow light flickered in the distance and a soft but chill breeze blew in and caressed their faces.

Her breathing then became laboured as she struggled with the bubbling mucous in her throat. She uttered no words.

She then pushed back into him as her body tensed and she gripped his hand tightly. Her final sigh then seemed to expel what was left of the force within her, and as it faded her body eased and seemed to melt back into his naked chest, and then he knew that she had gone.

Wanoka choked back the tears as she stroked the cold crossed hands of her stepmother. Serene in death Rosheen wore a cotton dress of her favourite pale blue and her hair framed her face in auburn ringlets. Her illness had reduced her once well-rounded body to a spare almost emaciated figure. Her china-white skin had become strangely translucent, and her lips were tinged with a faint purple hue.

Reflections of Wanoka's true mother were vague, disintegrated and mentally clouded by trauma, and were manifestations of a time-distorted memory of her mountain childhood. Rosheen, however, had become the bedrock and caring mentor of Wanoka's young life.

The news of her stepmother's passing had come hard and shocking, and Wanoka had travelled the long roads from Boston, accompanied by the worthy Rollo, reaching the inn a day before Rosheen was due to be laid to rest.

Rosheen had lain in her coffin for two days in a small room at the rear of the inn. She had always treated those who worked for her fairly and rewarded them well, and one by one they all paid their respects to the woman whom they had always respected and revered. She would be buried with her father and mother in the family grave on the land at the rear of the inn.

Before she was laid to rest Isaiah spent moments of reflection alone with her, standing beside her with his hand on her forehead. During his meditation, once again he sensed the gnawing void of absence that he had experienced when Rimmer died. However, curiously, he did not feel the haunting pull of a presence departing on the night

Rosheen had passed away, as he had experienced with the passing of Watseka.

Globules of cold moisture from a heavy morning mist settled on the hats and black-clad shoulders of the few mourners who stood and watched Rosheen's coffin being lowered into the family grave, and as it descended the words of the hymn *How Great Thou Art* flowed in crisp falsetto across the gathering. The voice of Wanoka drifted across the silent, dead, mist-laden land only to be lost in the grey echoing distance; a final farewell sung to a stepmother who had never failed her.

EPILOGUE

There was not a spare seat to be had at Crosby's Great Opera House in Chicago.

The interior of the huge theatre presented a wondrous vision of deep ruby and glimmering gold.

The discordant cacophony of instruments being tuned was backed by a shuffling low murmur, interrupted by the occasional cough, as the audience took their seats and waited in anticipation for the first performance of Giuseppe Verdi's latest opera, *Forza del Destino*.

The air hung heavy from the stifling summer night. Ladies' fans flickered like a sea of wings, and bewhiskered gentlemen removed their top hats.

Making her operatic debut singing the role of Donna Leonora was the soprano, Wanoka Stiener, and singing the role of Leonora's lover, Don Alvaro, was the young tenor, Rollo Simmons.

In the front row of the dress circle sat a tall but slightly stooped elderly man with thick, closely cropped sandy-grey hair.

His starched white cotton shirt and his finely tailored dark worsted suit did not hang well on him, and he frequently eased himself in his seat.

A finely wrought hawk's head cane leant against the back of the seat in front of him. A cold pipe hung from the side of his mouth and his eyes never left the great gold and maroon curtains that stretched across the dimly lit stage.

There was great applause as the conductor walked on from the wings and took his position on the podium.

As the curtains rose the overture pulsed in powerful waves through the space of the great auditorium.

For the next two hours surges of heart-pounding adrenalin transfixed the tall elderly man through act after act of tense drama and glorious singing.

Then in act four came the aria *Pace Pace Mio Dio*. The audience gasped at the power of the voice as it soared above the orchestra and reached sublime crescendos, and with every gesture and movement, every turn of the head, every sway of the hips enhanced by the light, the true mother of this voice seemed to emerge and then fade in intermittent waves with the power of the music, and then to the tall man, daughter and mother began to merge into one ethereal form, and then a searing light from above seemed to scorch all around and a shivering charge shot through his nerves, and numbness tugged at life's final throes, and then a soft whisper with a hint of mint and wild thyme caressed his neck and a savage beat of wings then drowned the great harmonies, and the scorching light beckoned and drew him on and on.

- THE END -

ACKNOWLEDGMENTS

The concept and ideas for this short novel have their roots in my life long obsession with the early American Frontier and the culture of the native Americans.

The idea for the story has simmered in my mind for a number of years and the general thread and flow of the narrative have slowly evolved through a process of writing.

Through an artist's eye, my travels across Wyoming, Colorado, Yellowstone and the Black Hills left me visually awe struck and in this novel I have attempted to use a style of prose as a kind of metaphor for visual images and sensations.

Powerful inspiration came from Cormac McCarthy's Masterpiece, Blood Meridian. I also have huge admiration for writers such as Ron Chernow and Hampton Sides. I would consider it a real achievement if my style of writing even approached their quality.

I owe a huge debt of gratitude to novelist and writer Sharn Hutton, whose guidance and advice was invaluable.

I would also like to mention Amanda Weakford of Bright VA for her excellent manuscript transcription and proof reading.

Printed in Great
Britain
by Amazon